The Cowboy Rescues a Bride

By Cora Seton

To my grandmother, who didn't let anyone keep her down.

The Cowboy Rescues a Bride is Volume 7 of the **Cowboys of Chance Creek** series, set in the fictional town of Chance Creek, Montana.

Chapter One

N ED MATHESON SHOVED his hands in the pockets of his thick, tan shearling work coat and hunched his shoulders against a strong wind sweeping east across the snow-covered pastures of the Double-Bar-K. The sun wasn't up yet on this January morning, and Montana winters were known for their brutality, but that wouldn't stop the animals that inhabited the ranch from waiting for him to tend to them.

He knew what it felt like to wait for something—and how good it felt to finally get it. After thirty-two long years of waiting, he was finally coming into his own. Finally taking charge of his family's cattle herd, after years of playing second fiddle to his older brother, Jake. He'd always known he was capable of running the family business—he was as good a judge of the stock as anyone, as cunning in negotiations, and he was the only one of his brothers who could repair all the equipment they used on the ranch as well as do all the other chores around the place. He should have been put in charge a long time ago. Instead, it took Jake coming to loggerheads with his father and moving onto his own acreage to clear the way for him.

None of that was on his mind, though, as his footsteps crunched over the frozen snow on his way to the barn. He wasn't paying attention to the cattle grouped over by the brush to the south in the home pasture, out of the wind, nor was it on the task ahead of him—hauling hay to a sheltered feed spot and making sure all the cattle were in good shape. Instead, he was thinking of a certain slim young woman with a dark, thick, waist-length braid, brown eyes that searched him out when she thought he wasn't paying attention, a low, musical voice that hooked his heart every time she spoke, and a sweet, curving mouth that hardly ever smiled, except when they were alone in his cabin.

He'd just left her there, in fact. Which sounded far more salacious than it was. Fila Sahar shared his cabin, but she hadn't shared his bed and he figured it would be a while before she did.

If ever.

He shook his head ruefully. That was frustration talking. They'd get there eventually. Fila just wasn't your run-of-the-mill young woman. You couldn't pick her up at a bar, take her out a few times and talk her into coming home for a little fun. Her circumstances made her different. When they were together it would be because he'd persuaded her to be together for good.

And he would persuade her of that.

Eventually.

"You're taking your time this morning."

His father's buzz-saw voice cut through his pleasant reverie and snapped his head up. Holt was leaning in the doorway of the trim red and white barn. Ned wondered how long he'd been there at the mercy of the cold, bitter wind. Why the hell was the man waiting out here?

"I talked to Ethan last night."

Ned knew he meant Ethan Cruz—their next door neighbor. The Cruzes had owned their ranch just about as long as the Mathesons had worked the Double-Bar-K. Two of the oldest ranching families in the county, the older generation had been something of rivals, but the younger generation got along just fine. Ned's youngest brother, Rob, was one of Ethan's best friends and a part-owner of the Cruz ranch, and Ned, Jake and Luke all went to the Cruz's Thursday night poker and pool games each week.

"What did he have to say?"

"His guests have all gone back home. The Big House is empty. They want Fila and Mia back."

Ned shouldered his way past his father into the barn and flicked on the lights. No need to have this conversation out in the dark and cold. Not that it was warm in here. Holt followed him inside. "Did you hear me?"

"I heard you. I don't think either of them wants to go back."

"I wasn't asking you. I was telling you."

Ned turned to face him. "You're telling me who can and can't live in my cabin?"

"I built that cabin for you."

Ned bit back a sharp retort. It was the least his father could do for all the work he'd done on this place. Knowing they'd each inherit a share of the ranch someday, he and his brothers had been content for years to work the spread in exchange for room, board and a small allowance. Lately, though, they'd come to realize the true cost of such an arrangement. Holt had always ruled their lives with an iron fist, but it wasn't until the last few months that he'd begun to interfere in their love lives. Jake and Rob were both married because of his interference, but both had managed to convince him to carve off a chunk of the spread for their very own. He'd figured he'd be the next one Holt tried to marry off.

So why kick out Fila? Ned was pretty sure he knew.

His father leaned closer. "She's not the one for you."

Ned stilled. "I say she is."

Holt's expression hardened. "I say she ain't. And you don't want to push me."

So this was how it was going to go. If he was truthful, Ned had expected it might, but he'd hoped against hope his father would surprise him. Holt Matheson was a man of contradictions. Since most folks in Chance Creek had known him all their lives, they knew that underneath his aggravating bluster lay a man who loved his family, his town and all of America. Those who didn't know him generally counted him a jackass. Ned understood his father's shades of gray. Holt counted on things staying within a strict framework that he understood. Whatever was native to Chance Creek was good. Whatever was foreign to it was bad. The more foreign it got, the worse it was to his way of thinking.

Which left Fila shit out of luck.

Despite Holt's classification system, Fila wasn't actually foreign. Born in Connecticut of Afghan parents, raised as American as apple pie for her first twelve years, she'd traveled to the country of her parents' birth to attend the funeral of her grandmother and there disaster had struck. The funeral procession was attacked by Taliban warriors, Fila's parents were killed in front of her, and she was taken captive. Raised in a remote Afghan mountain village for the next ten years, Fila did what she had to in order to survive. When her chance to escape came, she took it and made her way here—to the home of the woman whose organization, Aria's House, helped her return to the United States. Aria Cruz had already passed away, but her son, Ethan, and his wife, Autumn, took Fila in, gave her a home and a place to get back on her feet.

That made Fila as American as any of them.

But Holt couldn't see it. Especially when the Taliban men that had followed her to Chance Creek to retrieve her ended up shooting Rob in the shoulder before they were captured. Rob was fine—nearly fully recovered—but Holt couldn't forgive Fila her part in the incident. Ned was afraid he never would.

That didn't mean he was going to change his mind.

"You're the one who shouldn't push things." He met his father's steely gaze with one of his own. "She's the one I mean to marry. Best get used to it right now."

Holt's face changed color, but his tone remained steely. "You marry that girl and I'll cut you right out of my will. You will be dead to me!"

"Better start making funeral arrangements then." Ned turned on his heel and headed back toward the door, anger simmering throughout his bloodstream. "Make my casket walnut. I've always been partial to a walnut casket."

"Goddamn it!"

Ned slowed to a stop despite himself. That break in Holt's voice wasn't something he was accustomed to. He waited for more. He wasn't disappointed.

"I could accept a first-generation American. It's not what I want for my son but I could accept it. I could accept a woman who for all intents and purposes practices a different religion—"

"Fila's not all that religious—"

"That's why I said for all intents and purposes," Holt snapped. "I could even accept you falling for a girl that nearly got your brother killed, seeing as I doubt she meant for that to happen."

"No, I doubt she did."

Holt ignored his sarcasm. "But I cannot stand here and watch you hitch yourself to a damaged woman."

Ned stiffened. "What the hell do you mean by that?"

Holt must have caught his tone. Realized he'd gone too far. For once he explained himself. "I mean that girl can't hardly meet a man's eyes. She can't hardly walk out her door. She has no skills. She's frightened of her own shadow. What kind of partner is she going to be for you? You're going to be her nursemaid, not her husband. You think you can heal her? You can't."

Of all the things his father could have said, this was the one that cut him to the quick—because it was true. He did want to heal Fila. He thought he could. Holt's words highlighted his darkest fear.

Maybe Fila was beyond saving. Maybe she'd never confront her demons and win.

"Watching you marry that girl will be like watching you commit suicide. You can't ask that of me."

How the hell could he answer that?

Ned decided he couldn't. He walked out the door.

FILA HUMMED ALONG with the pop song playing on the iPod Ned had stationed in a dock on the kitchen counter this morning for her. She'd been able to find an online radio station that played hit music from the last decade—all the songs she'd missed while she'd been away. She was determined to learn them, to recapture her lost years. Pop music was one of the things she'd missed the most during her time in captivity.

She moved around the pleasant room quickly, gathering the ingredients she needed to make *bolani*—potato and green onion-filled flatbreads—one of Ned's favorite Afghan dishes. She loved this now-familiar space with its hardwood floors and trim, and the wide windows that looked out over the pastures to the south. At first she'd been terrified to move in with the silent cowboy who owned the house when Ethan and Autumn needed her bedroom for an influx of paying guests, but she'd soon found that Ned's brusqueness hid a tenderness she would never have credited in the man, especially since she'd heard the way everyone else talked about him. If she listened to gossip she'd think Ned was a fighter, but she'd never seen such a thing. Bringing her the iPod was just the latest in a long line of considerate gestures he'd made toward her.

As the song's chorus sounded, Fila tried to sing along, but the sound of her own voice ringing out in the otherwise quiet house brought her up short and had her glancing over her shoulder to see if anyone had heard. She dropped the measuring cup she'd begun to dip into the bag of flour and gripped the counter to keep herself on her feet as waves of fear and nausea spun over her frame. She gripped the inch-thick wood with both hands, fighting against the urge to run upstairs and hide in her bed, to wrap herself up in her quilts and huddle there until her breathing slowed again.

There was nothing here to fear. She was alone. She was safe.

The Taliban were thousands of miles away.

Probably.

No, definitely.

Fila straightened again. This was America. This was Chance Creek—not the hills of Afghanistan, where singing a pop song got you beaten—or your food withheld for two days. This was Chance Creek, where country music spilled from every radio, and listening to pop music—while not exactly approved of—was definitely tolerated. She made herself focus on the song again, already familiar with the words although it had come out during the time she was away. She waited for the chorus to come around again, then once more joined in, singing an entire phrase before her body reacted and shut her down. Her pulse increased, her breaths came short and quick as she gripped the counter harder. She braced herself for a slap or a pinch or a harsh volley of words, none of which came, of course.

She was safe. No one wanted to hurt her here.

Fila took deep breaths like Autumn had taught her—in through her nose and out through her mouth. Still the fear rolled over her, her stomach pitching and tossing like a ship on the waves. When she couldn't stand it anymore, she sunk to the floor to crouch on her knees, her fingers sliding from their handholds until she was balled up on the hard wood, her arms wrapped around her chest, her shoulder pressed against the cabinets that supported the butcher block island where she'd begun to work.

She fought back the tears that threatened to fall and swallowed past the burning lump in her throat. She couldn't even sing. The Taliban had taken that from her just like they'd taken everything else.

She couldn't sing, she couldn't laugh, she couldn't venture out past her front door without feeling like she'd pitch up the contents of her stomach at any moment.

Fear was her constant companion, just as it had ever been in the little village in Afghanistan. She'd thought she'd outrun it. She'd thought she'd conquered it during her flight home.

But it had followed her here and refused to give up its grip on her life.

She couldn't let it beat her. She couldn't let them win—those wiry men with piercing eyes and furious tempers, with their diatribes against everything and everyone and their need to hem her in, cut her down, dictate her every move, steal her words, steal her parents, steal her home—

Fila lurched to her feet again, damned if she would let them control her now. She leaned on the counter, not caring that the flour had tipped over, not caring that her clothes were dusted in white. She lifted her voice again, softly but at least out loud—at least audible, if only to her. She raised her voice again, catching the chorus as it came around a third time, pairing her words to the singer's, her tones to the melody coming out of the iPod dock.

As her hands shook, her stomach cramped and tears ran down her cheeks, she sang along until the song ran out. Then she dashed for the bathroom and heaved until her stomach was as empty as it ever was on a snowy day in the middle of the Hindu Kush mountains of northeastern Afghanistan.

Chapter Two

LUKE DROPPED AN envelope on Ned's workbench in his mechanics shed about a half hour before lunch. Taller than Ned, but somewhat slighter, he was barely a year younger than him. They'd been the middle ones, sandwiched between bossy Jake and trickster Rob. People liked to think of the Matheson boys as a unit—the way they'd appeared when they were kids forced by their mother to attend church. Four blond boys in a row like stairsteps, each a year apart from the next in line. Ned had separated himself from the others by his penchant for trouble. Luke had gone in the other direction. He was upright, a hard worker, rarely fussed or complained, and saw the whole world in terms of black and white. People had a tendency to forget about Luke. Ned knew part of his own hair-trigger temper when he was younger was a desire for people not to forget about him.

"Enjoy," Luke said and turned back to the door.

"What the hell is that?" Ned eyed the large envelope suspiciously.

"Feed supplement order. You place the order online, of course—that's just the catalog and a reminder of what we've ordered in the past.

"That's Mom's job."

"Jake did it until now."

"So give it to him." Ned turned his back on the envelope. Wasn't going to do him any good, since he couldn't read its contents.

"You're in charge of the herd, as you keep reminding all of us. So you're in charge of the feed supplement order." Luke walked out of the shop and slammed the door behind him.

Ned felt his anger flare. He knew damned well that Luke could send this order in if he wanted to. Jake had stepped down from managing the place so he could take classes at Montana State, but those hadn't even started yet. He could do it in a matter of minutes as a favor to them. If not him, then Rob or his mother, Lisa, could place the order.

Luke was deliberately giving him a hard time. This was his way of showing Ned that his grip on the reins of this operation was tenuous at best. Luke wanted the job as much as Ned had ever wanted it. Ned shook his head. He should have expected something like this. He wouldn't get help from Luke—or Rob or Jake, for that matter. His mother would be sympathetic, but going to her would open up a whole new can of worms. Would she try to convince him to sign up for tutoring again? Or drag him to one of those doctors she was always on about?

Lisa was the only one who didn't accept his dyslexia as a done deal. Everyone else in the family knew he couldn't read and never would. No one outside of his family knew about his difficulty at all.

He hoped.

A familiar tightness gripped his chest at that possibility, but he forced himself to remain calm. No one knew and no one would ever know. That was that. But his dyslexia had dogged him his entire life and he could see that taking charge of the ranch wasn't going to change anything. It might just make things worse.

In his younger days he'd used his fists to cover up his deficiencies. At school he was always fighting until he'd finally dropped out. As a young man, those fights continued. Nothing stopped questions faster than fear. He'd been feared for the power of his punches and his hair-trigger temper.

Funny how no one seemed to notice that he'd changed.

He was still ill-tempered some of the time, he'd grant them that. But when was the last time he'd used his fists? When was the last time Cab Johnson—the county sheriff— had dragged him home? When was the last time he'd given anyone any grief?

Except his brothers, who hardly counted.

And deserved it.

He'd stopped all that, thanks to a timely word from Cab himself about a year ago, when he lost Boomer, the last in a line of yellow labs that he'd favored since he was a kid. Boomer had been his best friend for years—the kind of dog that was never more than a few feet away from him unless he'd been ordered to stay while Ned left the ranch. The kind of dog that waited patiently for his return and leaped with happiness every time he did. The kind of dog that rode in the front seat of his truck on errands, lay at the end of his bed at night, and was alert to his every mood and movement from sunup to sundown. Boomer had loved him just because he was Ned. No questions asked. No judgments given. He'd been old and slowing down when Ned had lost him, but he would have lasted another year at least.

If Ned hadn't taken him to town, let him off the leash and turned his back. He didn't know why Boomer had seen fit to cross the road just as Henry Dillon took the corner of Main and First a little too fast. Boomer's end was swift—over before the dog could feel the pain.

But Ned had felt the pain.

He didn't know what happened next, except suddenly the baseball bat that had been rattling around in the bed of his truck for months was in his hands, and the windows of Henry's Chevy were all busted out, glass scattered far and wide across Main. Henry himself was backing away, his hands stretched out in supplication, pleading for him to come to his senses.

Just for a moment—just for one moment, Ned had considered what else he could do with that bat.

And then he saw his future as clear as day in one blinding flash of insight—the kind he rarely had in life. If he took this step it was good-bye ranch, good-bye family, good-bye cattle and pastures and horses and dawns breaking over a landscape so big it seemed God could hardly hold it in his hands.

Good-bye Sunday dinners at his parents' dining room table, good-bye Thursday poker and pool, good-bye aching shoulders and the peace that comes after a twelve-hour day in the mud and muck of a spring washout fixing a downed fence.

Good-bye newborn calves struggling to take their first wobbly steps toward their mothers' milk. Good-bye sunrises and sunsets and sunrises and sunsets, and all the days between that made up each year.

He'd dropped the bat just as Cab swerved around the corner in his sheriff's cruiser, stepped out and surveyed the scene.

He didn't want to give up his life—not any of it. He didn't want to hurt anybody, either. He couldn't walk this path anymore.

Cab must have seen something of his thoughts in his eyes. He should have arrested Ned and hauled him up to see a judge. With all his priors, Ned should have spent some time in jail.

Instead, Cab gripped his bicep with fingers that could have snapped his arm in two, stepped into Ned's personal space and said, "One more time."

Ned had nodded. He knew exactly what Cab meant. He had one more chance to get it right. One more chance to become the man he knew he could be. One more chance to learn another way of dealing with the heartbreak and pain life threw at you.

One more chance, or he'd be locked up for a good, long time.

Ned had grabbed that chance with two hands and was holding on for dear life. Especially now that Fila had come to Chance Creek.

He put his tools away carefully, tucked the envelope under his arm, and left the shop to make his way back to his cabin. He'd take a look at the contents when he was alone. Maybe he could piece together the information he needed from the catalog's pictures. Maybe he could read just enough of the words to figure it out.

Or maybe it would remain as much a mystery as a foreign language, he thought disgustedly.

Or maybe Fila could help.

With that thought buoying him up, he increased his pace, already anticipating the meal to come.

BY THE TIME Ned came through the door for lunch, Fila had herself under control again. She'd sobbed until she'd run out of tears, then taken a shower, scrubbed her face until it burned, washed her hair and rebraided it, got dressed in clean clothes and tried again.

This time she didn't sing along to the music, but she kept it on, absorbing the words and rhythms and melodies, hoping against hope that they would crowd out the haunting Afghan tunes that had filled her head for the past decade.

She still managed to have the *bolani* ready for Ned's meal when he came home from morning chores. He burst through the door in a wash of cold, fresh air that braced her up.

"Be right there." He tossed a large envelope on the sofa in the living room, kicked off his boots, hung up his jacket and cowboy hat and headed for the bathroom. A few minutes later they were seated at the table, and Fila served him several *bolani* flatbreads and passed a container of spiced yogurt to use as a dip.

As she sat down in her chair, she felt Ned's gaze on her and she knew he had noticed the signs of her earlier tears by the way his mouth went hard. He didn't say anything, though. Just fell to eating with a relish that made her heart warm. Ned liked her cooking. He liked the way she kept his home. He did a million little thoughtful things to show her that he was pleased.

He never, ever yelled or hit or pinched or punched—no matter what she did. Fila knew that was supposed to be a given, but it wasn't. Not in her experience.

"I had to feed the cattle twice as much as usual this morning. Sure is cold out there."

Fila nodded. She'd seen the cattle come out from their sheltered hideouts in the brush to eat their hay this morning. They'd stood patiently in the uncomfortable weather and eaten their fill. Ned had explained that digesting the tough hay actually helped increase their body temperatures.

"We're still on for dinner tonight, aren't we?"

Fila set the piece of flatbread she was eating down on her plate and wiped her hands on the napkin that lay across her lap. She'd hoped Ned would forget about that.

"Yes," she said finally, but she dreaded the outing.

"It'll be great, you'll see," Ned said. "The food at Del-Monaco's is terrific. Almost as good as yours."

She tried to smile.

"Besides, I want to show you something. Something you're really going to like."

"What?" Her voice was thin and she wanted to try again, but that seemed silly. She knew she had to practice talking as much as she needed to practice singing, though, so she cleared her throat. "What do you want me to see?"

"It's a surprise," Ned said. "You'll like it, though. I know it." He held up a flatbread. "These are terrific, like always. My favorite."

"I know."

"The house looks great. What are you going to do this afternoon?"

Fila shrugged. The usual. Listen to her music. Watch television. Autumn had encouraged her to watch as much as she could to catch up with everyone else after her ten year absence. She was beginning to understand pop culture again and while she found she had to avoid the news and violent dramas or risk flashbacks, she enjoyed women's talk shows and had even gotten hooked on a soap opera. It passed the time and made her feel like she had company, even if in reality she was alone.

Sometimes Ned's mother came over for a chat, or invited her over to the main house on the spread to spend time there, but Lisa seemed to understand that made her feel uncomfortable. The older women in the village she'd left behind were sometimes as bad as the men. Or worse. Lisa was so kind and sweet, Fila hated herself for the way her words dried up in her throat around her. Her reaction was yet another indication of how much her fear had a hold on her. Fila knew she was healing, bit by bit and step by step.

She just hadn't expected it to take so long.

"There's something you could do for me," Ned said, breaking into her thoughts. "That envelope over there has some information about feed supplements we need to order for the cattle. I don't have time to look through it today. Think you might take a look? It'd be a help."

Understanding broke over Fila. He wanted her to read through it because he couldn't.

It hadn't taken her long to discover Ned's secret, once she'd come to live with him. It had been the clue to all that anger and ill-temper everyone else talked about. Ned was a proud man, just like the village men had been back in Afghanistan, and just like them he hated to feel at a disadvantage in any way.

Just like many of them, he couldn't read.

Fila had missed reading even more than she missed music when she was in Afghanistan, but while she learned to speak Pashto during her time there, she had no opportunity to learn to read it. There was very little in the village to read, and what little there was wouldn't have been shared with her. She soon realized that ignorance of the wider world was deemed becoming in a woman. Education wasn't. Fila kept her mouth shut and learned to play dumb. She paid attention, though. She knew what a man looked like when he couldn't read but wanted to pretend he did. She'd seen Ned act the same way soon after she arrived on the ranch. It didn't take long to put two and two together. While many Afghan village men might be illiterate, few American men were. She realized the disadvantage Ned was under. Saw how hard he worked to cover it up.

Understanding his secret made the rest of his behavior easy to decipher. And since she didn't expect Ned to read, she didn't inadvertently put him into embarrassing situations.

So he relaxed and showed his true nature. Which turned out to be kind of wonderful.

If she could help him in any way in return, she'd certainly do so. "I will read it," she said, serving him another piece of *bolani*.

Ned tore a chunk off and dipped it into the yogurt sauce. "Thanks."

Chapter Three

N ED PARKED HIS truck near the corner of First Street
and Main, and hurried to the door of a storefront
whose windows were covered up with butcher paper. He
let himself in and shut the cold out behind him, blowing on
his hands. Warm air washed over him, along with voices
from the back of the building. He looked around in
satisfaction at the newly refurbished interior.

"Well, what do you think?" Jake said, pushing a broom
around the tables and chairs that filled the front half of the
small establishment. "They look good, don't they?"

Ned knew he was referring to the tables, which Jake
had built himself. Their natural wooden surfaces were
beautiful, as were the booths he'd fashioned to fit along the
length of one interior wall. Jake had surprised Ned when he
volunteered to help, and he knew he had Morgan—Rob's
wife—to thank for that. All he'd done was mention to her
in passing what he meant to do for Fila and she got
everyone else on board. Rob had helped Jake with the
tables. Hannah, Jake's wife, and Mia, who was currently
living with Luke, had discovered a set of chairs at an estate
sale and figured out how to reupholster them. Mia enlisted

her friend Rose from the Cruz ranch to help pick a palette of warm colors for the walls, upholstery and other decorative elements. They had debated long and hard about how to theme the restaurant. It was obvious that Fila loved the food of the country her parents came from, but her time in captivity had left deep scars—something she didn't need to be reminded of each day when she came to work.

Rose, an artist, had suggested they use colors and abstract shapes to give the restaurant an exotic feel, while not using specific details that might call to mind unhappy times. She used earthy reds, yellows and oranges to make the space feel warm, upbeat and inviting. They decided that Fila would add her own touches over time to make the restaurant truly her own.

Rob had installed large chalkboard panels behind the counter where Fila could put up a menu and specials. Rose had created a beautiful chalk border for it, swirling dancing designs around its edges. The restaurant was meant to be a casual eatery, where guests placed their orders and paid at the counter, then found seats for themselves.

Ned had cleaned, serviced and polished every kitchen appliance to a shine. He'd built shelves to hold Fila's ingredients and placed racks and hooks in every conceivable space to make the storage of pots, pans and utensils as convenient as possible.

Rob had also installed the speaker system, linked to an iPod dock he'd set up in the kitchen. He'd found a site that featured contemporary pop music and was legal for restaurants to play for their customers. The cost was minimal and it would add to the atmosphere. When someone suggested a world music station, Ned had shaken his head. Pop music was important to Fila. She'd missed a decade of it during the years she was abroad and now she was making up for lost time.

Morgan had offered to help design Fila's promotional materials once Fila was ready for them. She'd already designed a logo for the restaurant, which Jake had carved onto a large wooden sign. The rest would have to wait until Fila had made her menu choices.

Activity ceased in the restaurant as one by one the workers noticed Ned's return.

"What do you think? Is everything ready?" Morgan asked him, coming out of the kitchen. Mia followed her, her long, dark ponytail swinging.

Ned looked around at the cheerful room with its tables and chairs, the shining counter and display cases that separated the restaurant from the back rooms, the large chalkboard waiting for a menu and the gleaming kitchen through the swinging doors just waiting for its cook.

"I think it's perfect," Ned declared. "She's going to love it."

A sharp rap on the door had all of them turning to face it.

"Wonder who that is?" Jake said.

Ned crossed to open it and found a woman he'd never seen before on the other side. His first impression was that she reminded him of Fila. Slim and a good eight inches shorter than him, she had long, dark hair, expressive eyes and a south of the border skin tone. Unlike Fila, her hair flowed unbound in wild waves around her shoulders, and her lips were painted a dramatic red.

"Hola!" Her voice reverberated off the small restaurant's walls as she pressed past Ned and came inside. Nothing shy about her at all, he noted. She wore skinny jeans, high heels and a sweater that hugged every curve, emphasizing her womanliness without coloring her cheap. Her smile was wide as she took in the bright décor and the shine of the display cabinets and countertop. "It looks wonderful! You've done a great job!" The woman had just a trace of an accent, which made them all lean forward to catch her words. "I'm Camila Torres. I'm next door." She waved her hand at the windowless side wall. When no one spoke she elaborated. "I've leased the storefront next door. I'm opening a restaurant, too!"

"You're opening a restaurant?" Ned said. The muscles in his neck tightened. Competition for Fila? That was the last thing she needed.

"Si! Yes! Mexican, with a twist. I add a little of this and a little of that—sometimes I serve traditional dishes. Sometimes I make up something new." She cocked her head and smiled. "And which of you is Fila?"

"None of us." Jake moved forward and offered his hand to shake. "I'm Jake Matheson. This is my brother, Ned. My wife Hannah and sister-in-law Morgan. My friends Mia and Rose. We're all helping prepare the place as a surprise for another of our friends."

"For Fila?" Camila flashed a bright smile. "I can't wait to meet her. She is a her, isn't she?"

"Yes, she is." Hannah came forward to greet her. "Her specialty is Afghan cuisine."

Camila sucked in a breath, her whole face lighting up in surprise. "Afghan food, here in Chance Creek! Then I'm not exiled to the far wastes of civilization, after all!"

There was a moment of silence at this surprising declaration. Camila laughed, long and loud at their expressions.

"I've lived in Houston, Texas for the last eight years. Before that I grew up in Mexico City. I have always been surrounded by hustle and bustle. Then I came here and"—

she waved an expressive hand again—"nothing. I live out on the Flying W and I open my door and see"—she shrugged—"nothing! Where is everyone?"

Rose laughed. "I can see how Chance Creek would be a bit of a shock after Houston and Mexico City. You'll get used to it, though. There's plenty to see and do here. The trick is making good friends."

Camila flashed Ned a big smile. "Then I hope I'm well on my way to making a good start."

"HOW ABOUT THIS one?" Autumn pulled a long wool skirt in muted earth tones out of Fila's closet. "You could pair it with this sweater." She held up a cream-colored cashmere one. A small, sparrowlike woman normally, now her pregnant belly was large enough to make her clumsy. Fila appreciated that she'd come to help.

"Okay." Fila brushed out her hair and prepared to re-braid it.

"You could leave your hair down," Autumn suggested. She'd been the one to take in Fila after she arrived in Chance Creek and she knew without Fila having to explain anything that she dreaded her meal with Ned at the restaurant, but she was doing her best to soothe Fila and help her find the courage to go through with it.

"Why don't you tell Ned how you feel?" she'd asked when she'd first come over. Fila had just shaken her head and Autumn didn't push her to explain. Ned had been so kind. He had given her a home, fed her—supported her. Surely she could make it through one dinner in return.

Fila regarded her reflection in the mirror. She knew to anyone in Chance Creek a hairstyle was just a hairstyle, but where she'd spent the last ten years it meant so much more.

It was hard enough to sit out in public and eat with a man. Hard enough to walk from truck to restaurant without wrapping herself in a burka. Hard enough to expose herself in a way that still felt dangerous, even after all these months.

But to wear her hair spread over her shoulders like a common—

Fila turned away. "I prefer it up."

"Okay." Autumn hung the clothes on the handle of the closet. "I brought something for you, though. I think it will go perfectly with your outfit." She pulled a small, square box out of her pocket and handed it to Fila. "Open it up!"

Fila did, to find a simple, but elegant pendant inside. Autumn was right; it would go with her outfit beautifully, and there was nothing flashy about it. Nothing that made Fila feel in danger.

"Thank you," she said to Autumn.

"Get changed. I want to see it on."

Ten minutes later Fila surveyed herself in the mirror again. She knew she looked old-fashioned with her pinned up hair and pretty, but proper outfit. She wore a pair of plain cowboy boots with her skirt, so she'd fit in at Del-Monaco's. As Autumn had told her with a smile, "You can wear any outfit with a pair of boots and you'll be just fine."

Autumn checked the time. "I better go. Ned will be here soon and he won't appreciate me intruding into your time with him."

When Fila turned to her in surprise, Autumn just shook her head. "You can't tell me you haven't noticed—that man is sweet on you. I'd bet my last dollar on it."

Fila walked her to the door, too surprised to even say good-bye. Ned? Sweet on her?

She bit back a smile.

Chapter Four

NED KNEW FILA had been reluctant to come to DelMonaco's with him, but first he meant to wine and dine her, and then he'd take her to see her surprise. The others would meet them at her restaurant at seven-thirty. He couldn't wait to see Fila's face when she saw what they had done. She seemed nervous now, glancing around the busy dining room and fiddling with the napkin in her lap. She was always a little jittery in crowds. He figured she'd settle in once their meals came. He'd ordered them both steaks, baked potatoes and salad with the house dressing, and he'd encouraged her to try one of the dinner rolls that Sarah-Jane, their waitress, had left on the table.

Fila pulled off a chunk of the roll and nibbled at it nervously, her gaze skidding around the room from one table to another of boisterous eaters. Ned had never realized how loud it got in DelMonaco's—Chance Creek's most popular restaurant. Fila was as tightly strung as a deer waiting to bound away to safety. When Fila had first arrived in town, all everyone could talk about was how brave she'd been to escape her captors. Then when she'd been pursued, she'd shown great courage again, trying to trade her own life for the safety of all the others who were there at the shootout.

After the danger was past, though, Fila seemed to collapse in on herself. Then Federal agents had arrived and demanded to question her about her time in Afghanistan, the men who had followed her to Montana and what her ties to them might still be. The questioning had lasted for several days. The Fila who emerged after it was a pale shadow of the woman she'd previously been. Autumn had explained it to him at one of the Cruz's Thursday poker and pool nights.

"She thought she was coming home—that she'd be safe the minute she touched down on American soil. That's what kept her together through her travels. But first those Taliban men hunted her down and showed her she wasn't safe—even here. And then those Federal agents rounded her up and questioned her like she was an enemy. They had to do it, of course," Autumn hurried on. "For all they knew the Taliban had planted her here for a reason, but it's…broken her, Ned. She's just…lost."

His fingers twitched at the memory—wanting to ball themselves into fists—but he made himself relax them and return his attention to Fila. "Quite a crowd, isn't it?"

Fila nodded.

"Lots of business. People love to eat out." He was building up to his purpose for bringing her here, but now that they were at the restaurant, he wasn't sure how to proceed. At home Fila seemed like she was making progress every day. She had a quiet confidence when she worked in her kitchen. Here she had shrunk into herself in a way that made him nervous for her. He decided not to push it now. "It was a pleasant day today."

Fila's eyebrows shot up. The temperature had hardly climbed out of the single digits and the wind hadn't let up all day.

"For January," Ned amended. He searched for another topic of conversation. "That stuff you made yesterday was really good. That meat dish."

"Thank you."

"You cook just as well as the people here do."

Fila smiled a little and his heart rose—she'd been so tense since they'd left the cabin. "But I don't do steaks."

"No. Not yet, anyhow. I bet you'll get the hang of it someday. If you want to." He was relieved when Sarah-Jane, their waitress, delivered their salads. He felt like he was making a mess of things. Somehow back at home when he'd been planning what to say, it had all made sense. At least in his mind. Fila needed something to occupy her time. She needed to feel like she had something to offer the town, and she needed to earn an income so she wouldn't feel at the mercy of everyone else. All of these things would increase her confidence and help her heal. "Still, I like your cooking because it's different, you know? You can't get anything like it in Chance Creek."

Fila shrugged.

"In fact, I've had an idea—a way you can earn the money you need." This was it. Make or break time. Would Fila see the possibilities? Would she be overwhelmed with gratitude for the opportunity he was presenting her?

She froze in the act of lifting a forkful of salad to her mouth. Placed it down again carefully and folded her hands in her lap. She didn't look grateful. She looked terrified. "A way to earn money?" she echoed quietly.

Ned took a breath. Here's where he put his cards on

the table. Where he showed how much he cared about her and the lengths to which he'd go to make her happy. This was the first step in the journey towards making her his wife, no matter what his father said. "Yeah. I know you've been worried about it, but I've got it all figured out."

She stared at him.

"You can open your own restaurant!"

FILA FOUGHT THE urge to be sick. Open a restaurant? That was Ned's solution to her problems? She clutched the edge of the table to keep the room from spinning. She'd barely managed to make it here. Her heart had been in her mouth since they left the cabin. And he thought she should open a restaurant?

"Well? What do you think?"

Ned was obviously thrilled with the idea. Fila searched for the right words to explain why that was impossible. Why it was unthinkable.

"A restaurant?" she managed to say. She felt like her throat would close up any minute. Her palms were sweating and a fine tremble had started in her limbs. Did he not understand how hard it had been to climb in his truck and drive the five miles to town? Didn't he know she shook whenever she felt the large Montana sky above her? That coming to a public place—among a crowd of strangers—left her so filled with panic that she wanted to run and hide?

Had he no sense of the fact that the only reason she had made it this far was that he had asked her to—and she couldn't repay his kindness with disrespect? She had no idea how she would get through the rest of this meal, let alone open a restaurant and face the public every day of her life.

It was so far from possible as to be a joke.

Except Ned wasn't joking.

"A small restaurant," he explained. "Nothing overwhelming. You'd hire someone else to run the front end—to serve the customers and take their payments. You'd be in the kitchen, where you like to be. It would be great! I bet you'd make a killing, too. You'd have all the money you wanted."

He sat back, satisfied.

He couldn't have hurt her more if he'd taken out a pistol and shot her in the chest. "That takes money." She seized on an easy way out. She had no money—not yet. Maybe not ever. Autumn was helping her search to see if her parents had left anything behind when they died, but after a decade, Fila figured it was all gone.

"Don't worry about that—I'll handle everything." Ned looked pleased as punch. And why not? He thought he'd figured everything out.

She shook her head. "I will not take money from you."

"You've taken free rent—why wouldn't you accept a loan?"

Fila recoiled like he'd slapped her. She knew she was a burden on everyone. It pressed upon her every minute of every day. She knew she owed people more money than she could hope to pay off, but how could she work if she could barely leave the house? It was impossible. She didn't want to be a burden, but venturing out into public life, trying to start a business? She had no idea how to even begin to do that.

Plus she had the education of a twelve-year-old. She might be twenty-two, but she'd gone to Afghanistan in the middle of seventh grade and hadn't attended a day of classes since. She had no skills. She couldn't keep records or order supplies. She knew nothing about running a restaurant.

Sarah-Jane delivered their plates. "You two want anything else?"

Fila watched the young woman toss her head confidently. Sarah-Jane had no problem walking up to complete strangers and taking their orders, talking and laughing with them, presenting them with a bill. She could never do that. Just thinking about it made her want to hide.

"We're fine," Ned told her. He reached out and touched Fila's hand. She fought the urge to snatch it back. "It's a done deal, no need to argue. I won't take no for an answer."

He turned his attention to his meal and Fila gazed at her steak and potato miserably. He wouldn't take no for an answer. And how could she say no when she owed him so much? Until she could support herself—until she could pay everyone back—she would remain a burden forever.

She didn't think she could force a forkful of steak down her throat, but she made herself think of all the children in Afghanistan who would go to bed hungry tonight and took a bite. The handsome cowboy across the table deserved better than the reaction he was getting from her.

"How's your steak?" Ned asked brightly.

She forced herself to swallow. "Very good," she said and took a sip of water. Unshed tears stung her eyes. She wanted to go home. Wanted to go to bed and bury her face in the covers. Wanted to cry herself to sleep.

"It's not as good as your cooking. You're going to be a star."

Chapter Five

B Y THE TIME Ned led Fila out of DelMonaco's he was beginning to think he might have made a mistake. Fila hadn't eaten much of her dinner and as the meal went on, she seemed to shrink into herself more and more. A rowdy guest at another table had knocked a water glass to the ground and Fila nearly jolted out of her chair at the unexpected noise. Ned figured he might have over-estimated her readiness for rejoining public life. He recalled now that she'd even been overwhelmed by the poker and pool nights at Autumn's place. Even surrounded by friends, the loud voices and boisterous laughter seemed to press on her. Normally she slipped away before they were half over. At the last one, however, she'd managed to stay until it was done. That was weeks ago, though—before the houseful of paying guests had descended on Ethan and Autumn and she, Hannah and Mia had been forced to abandon the rooms they'd been renting and come to live on the Double-Bar-K.

Now those paying guests had left. Would Fila want to move back to Autumn's? He had to launch this new venture with her before that happened, or he was sure he'd lose her for good. All of Autumn's coddling wasn't helping Fila. She couldn't hide forever because of what had happened in the past. She needed to strike out on her own, try new things, get out of the house. His restaurant idea was the perfect vehicle. Once she'd found her footing and gained some confidence, she'd realize she really was safe here in Chance Creek. Her old fears would fall away and she'd be ready to look to the future.

She'd be ready to throw in her lot with him.

He was determined the night wouldn't be a failure. Out on their own on the quiet street, he touched her arm.

"I have something to show you. Do you mind a short walk? It will only take a minute."

Fila's eyes nearly begged him to take pity on her and take her straight home, but she nodded after a moment, hunching her shoulders into her thick winter coat. "Okay."

Her reaction added to his uneasiness, but he soldiered on and led her along the deserted sidewalk down a block and around the corner. "I know this isn't on the main drag, but it's still a good location," he said, stopping in front of the small storefront. A door was tucked into an indent between its large plate-glass windows which allowed them to stand out of the wind while Ned unlocked it.

"Where are we going?" Fila asked as she followed him inside. He flicked a light switch on and a crowd of people leaped up from their hiding places—all those who'd worked on the restaurant and the rest of their friends from the Cruz ranch and Double-Bar-K, too.

"Surprise!"

Fila gasped and fell back against him. Ned gripped her biceps to hold her upright.

"Well? What do you think?" He gestured to the warm,

inviting interior as the others looked on expectantly. The four couples who partnered on the Cruz ranch stood among the tables and chairs in the restaurant's seating section. Autumn and Ethan Cruz were the closest, Autumn's hands folded over her enormous pregnant belly, a slightly anxious expression on her face. Claire and Jamie Lassiter stood behind them, both of them grinning. Morgan and Rob perched on one of the booths and Rose and Cab Johnson leaned against another one.

Jake had positioned himself behind the counter with Hannah tucked under his arm. Luke and his housemate, Mia, were by the cash register. Ned knew for a fact Mia hoped Fila would hire her to run the front end of the restaurant.

Fila seemed dazed. "I don't know," she said finally, turning around in a circle. "What is it?"

"It's your restaurant." Ned took her hands in his. This was his moment. This was when Fila would realize how he felt about her—what he'd do to make her happy. "I paid the first six months' rent out of my savings and I have more to use for your startup costs. Everyone helped out. Ethan made the sign out front—I'll turn on the floodlights and you'll see it when we go out again. Jake made the tables and booths. The ladies painted and decorated. Everyone pitched in one way or the other."

She stood stock-still as he listed the names of everyone who'd lent a hand. He hoped Fila understood that she was surrounded by people that cared for her and they all wanted to help her succeed. "We called it Fila's." He squeezed her small hands in his. "You know there isn't anything I wouldn't do for you, don't you? I want for you to feel like Chance Creek is your home—like you have a place here. Everyone wants you to feel that way. What do you think?"

Fila still didn't move, and the unease that had been growing within him since they'd arrived at DelMonaco's surged up a notch. Fila stood as still as a statue—

Except for the tear that slid down her cheek.

Ned's stomach sank. "Fila?"

She drew in a shaky breath. In fact she was trembling all over.

"Fila? Sweetheart?" He dropped his voice so the others wouldn't hear.

Her gaze flashed to his at the endearment. Her eyes were wide, her lips parted. Tears snaked down her cheeks silently. Was that fear in her eyes? As Autumn and Rose raced to comfort her, the truth of it hit him like a cold, hard slap to his face.

He'd blown it. He'd blown everything.

Fila wasn't ready to start a restaurant—she could barely venture out his front door. She wasn't ready to supervise other workers—she could barely speak to anyone.

She wasn't in love with him, either.

Why would she be? He was a rough and tumble cowboy. A fighter.

An idiot.

Ned dropped her hands and backed away until he felt the handle of the door at his back. He was always blowing it. He was good for nothing. Hell, he'd scared the woman he loved. Filled with self-loathing, he yanked the door open, rushed through it and slammed it behind him. Outside, he paced in circles on the sidewalk, his anger only spiraling higher. He was such an idiot—a goddamned idiot. How could he make such a mistake?

The door opened behind him and Jake strode out. "It

isn't your fault and it's not over," he said.

"The hell it isn't. You saw her!"

"I saw a girl who's trying to put her life back together. I saw someone who's overwhelmed in the moment, but like you always say, she's a fighter. She'll pull through. Give her time to get used to the idea and she'll come to love it."

"I wanted her to love it now." *I wanted her to love me now.* He kept that last thought to himself. Jake wouldn't understand.

"She'll never love it if you don't get back in there and show her why she should."

Ned came to a halt. What the hell did that mean?

"Get back inside," Jake told him, pulling the door open again. "Get yourself under control and give her the grand tour."

FILA USED EVERY trick she'd ever learned to stop her tears and bring her emotions back under control. She imagined herself a pillar of stone. Impassive. Enduring. Untouched by even the winds that scoured the mountains in the worst of storms.

Stones don't cry.

How often had she told herself that during the years she was away? Stones don't cry. They can't be hurt. They can be weathered, but never changed. She had become stone during those years. She had remained standing no matter what they'd thrown at her.

She could do it again today.

She had to do it again today; she couldn't let these people who loved her down.

As Autumn and Morgan crowded around her, she rubbed her sleeve across her eyes and forced a smile to her lips. "It's beautiful," she said, pressing down against the swirl of terror that threatened to overwhelm her. "I can't believe you did all this for me." Her fake smiles elicited real smiles of relief as all her friends relaxed again.

The front door opened and Jake came back in, followed by a subdued Ned. As he approached, she made herself smile up at him too, knowing he had tried to help, no matter how far he'd gone astray.

This is a good man, she told herself. *This is a man who cares.* But she found herself wishing for her burka again, wanting to slip into a crowd of blue-clad bodies and disappear.

"I'm sorry if I pushed you. You don't have to run a restaurant." He stood with his fists shoved in his pockets.

Fila shook her head vehemently. "It's wonderful." Her voice was strained, but as clear as she could make it. "I am so grateful."

"I don't want your gratitude, I want—" He cut off. "I want you to be happy. I want you to feel like this is your home. Here in Chance Creek."

Tears pricked her eyes again, but this time there was joy mixed in with her sorrow. Somehow this cowboy cared for her—a warped, battered woman who was so far from whole as to be barely functional. What could he possibly see in her to make her worth his while? Whatever it was, she had to live up to it.

"We'll all keep helping you," Mia said. "Everyone wants to help you be a success."

Fila just nodded. What could she say?

"Grab a table, everyone." Morgan took charge. "Let's show her what it will look like when it's up and running."

"I'll man the cash register," Mia called out and nearly bounced to take her place at the till.

The rest of her friends found places at the tables and in

the booths as Fila watched them, clutching her hands tightly together. When there was someone at almost every table they turned to her. Their expressions were hopeful—like children waiting for praise.

"Well? What do you think?" Jake said, grinning widely.

For one brief second Fila could picture it. The tables crowded with talking, laughing patrons, music filling the air, the aroma of Afghan cooking wafting from the kitchen, Mia chatting up a customer at the till.

The vision rang so real and so true that for one moment she thought she could do it. Her heart surged. She could be a part of this. She could feed these people. She could stir her love and thankfulness and gratitude into every bite she put on their plates. She took in Ned's hopeful expression, the worry and hope warring in his eyes. She could do this, with his help. With everyone's help.

"Yes," she said. "It's wonderful."

As the room erupted in cheers and whoops, Ned swooped her into his arms, lifted her off her feet and twirled her around. "I knew you'd love it!" He pulled her close and kissed her on the mouth.

The cheering cut off abruptly. Fila's breath caught. Ned pulled back, seemed to realize what he'd done, and let go.

Fila staggered back until Hannah caught her. The room tilted under her feet, as the rest of their friends broke into an excited chatter.

"Fila?" Ned leaned toward her again. "Fila? Are you all right?"

She tried to nod, but her head spun too much to manage it. She saw him bend down, saw the floor come up to meet her.

Then everything went dark.

Chapter Six

"**I**'VE NEVER SEEN a man knock a woman out cold with a kiss before," Jake said to Ned. They were sitting in the living room of his cabin while Hannah tucked Fila into her bed. She'd revived quickly at the restaurant, but it was apparent to everyone the party was over for the night. He'd brought her straight home while the others had closed up the place. Jake, Hannah, Luke and Mia had followed right after him to help.

"I thought the kiss was supposed to wake the girl up," Luke drawled. "Fila's like a reverse Sleeping Beauty. Or maybe you're just not the right prince."

"Luke!" Mia elbowed him.

Ned surged to his feet and paced the cramped room. He wanted to be Fila's prince, but Jake and Luke were right—it wasn't going so well.

"She'll be fine. We should have known that surprising her wasn't very smart," Jake said.

They all looked up as Hannah came down the stairs.

"She's resting." Hannah sat by Jake and leaned against him. He twined his fingers with hers and Ned squashed a rush of jealousy. Jake and Rob both had wives who loved them. Luke would win Mia over sooner or later by the looks of things. Why was he the one life never worked out for?

"Give her time," Jake said.

Hannah smiled up at him. "That was some kiss."

With an impatient sound, he strode to the kitchen, trying to shut out Hannah and Mia's giggles. Why, oh why had he kissed Fila in front of everyone? Bad enough that she didn't want him—now everyone knew all about it.

"We'll keep gathering pots and pans and dishes for the restaurant," Hannah called after him. "I still think it's a great idea, Ned. You just have to be patient."

Sure. He could be patient. Ned opened the refrigerator and grabbed a beer. Struggled with an urge to dash it onto the floor.

Maybe.

FILA WAS UP before Ned the next morning. She slipped downstairs on silent feet, showered, dressed, checked her reflection in the mirror until she was sure all was right.

Ned had kissed her.

He'd kissed her.

Autumn was right; the tall, wonderful cowboy was sweet on her. And what had she done to show her appreciation for the fact that he took her to dinner, leased her a restaurant, renovated it—and kissed her?

She'd fainted dead on the floor.

Probably not the reaction he'd hoped for.

She'd tossed and turned all night thinking about that kiss, about the brush of his lips against hers, the heat and desire behind it. In that instant she'd gotten a flash of what it could be like with Ned—the passion he could show her, the spark that could kindle between them.

It scared her to death.

It set her on fire.

He had already grown to be special in her eyes. She knew he showed her a side of himself he showed to few others. That was fitting since he saw things about her no one else knew. Who else brought out her shy sense of humor? Who else knew how much she loved music?

Who else would look at her and see something worth caring for?

She'd given him a shoddy return for all his efforts. This morning she meant to show him that she knew what he'd tried to do and that she appreciated it.

She'd cooked an omelette, toast and sausage for breakfast by the time Ned got to the table. She could see by the rings under his eyes that he hadn't slept well, either. A pang of self-blame struck her at the realization that it was due to her.

"Morning," he said when he took in the table set with two places, the pitcher of fresh orange juice and plate fixed with his breakfast.

"Good morning," she said clearly. "Would you like some toast?" She was determined to live up to the courage he saw in her. She'd begin by speaking up instead of mincing her words like a frightened child.

"Sure thing."

As she passed him the plate, she took her own seat and faced him boldly across the table. It was still hard to look anyone in the eye, let alone a man, but she knew this was important. "I am sorry about last night. I was so surprised."

"I'm the one who should say I'm sorry. It was stupid.

All of it. I see that now and I'll do what I can to get rid of the place."

Fila stilled. "Get rid of it?"

"You're not ready to run a restaurant and I don't ever want to make you uncomfortable. You'll always have a home here. You know that, right? I won't force you to work and I sure as hell won't force you to—you know."

She stared at him until comprehension came. He was talking about the kiss. He wasn't going to do that again? Loss struck her like a punch to the gut. "I want to run a restaurant." The words blurted out of her mouth on their own accord.

Ned put down his fork. "I mean it, Fila. You don't have to work. You don't owe me anything."

"I want to," she said. And suddenly she realized it was true. She did want to. She wanted to earn an income. She wanted to stand on her own two feet.

She wanted to be the kind of woman Ned wanted to kiss.

"Are you sure?" His brow furrowed. He didn't believe her.

"I'm sure. It—it will be hard," she confessed. "But I want to."

"Okay." He bent over his meal again as if content to leave things there. It wasn't enough for Fila, though. That wasn't all she wanted, but she didn't know how to say the rest. Couldn't say it to a man.

Instead, she reached out and touched Ned—just a finger to the back of his hand. She pulled her hand back almost as soon as they connected.

He froze. Looked at her. Put his utensils down.

Slowly reached out and took her hand.

And held it.

FILA THOUGHT HER heart would thump right out of her chest. He was touching her. Holding her hand.

She was letting him.

Her breathing had gone ragged. Tears pricked her eyes for a reason she barely understood. If he moved or tried anything she would have to break and run, but he didn't move. Not a millimeter. She was beginning to think he understood her better than she understood herself.

"You can still say no." Ned's gaze was direct, but not frightening.

Did he mean to the restaurant? Or to what was happening between them now?

"I don't want to say no." She couldn't pinpoint what changed in his expression at her answer. Not a muscle moved in his face, but she felt his satisfaction. A moment later he let go of her hand and they resumed eating their breakfasts, but Fila knew that everything had changed between them. She had taken his challenge—to reenter the world, to meet him halfway. Now there was no going back.

"Where do you want to spend the morning? Here? Or at the restaurant?" Fila swallowed hard at his questions. "I could drop you at the restaurant with your laptop. I got an internet connection hooked up for you. You could take notes on everything you want to do. Start thinking about a menu, maybe? Morgan said something about you needing to take a food safety course or two. She thinks you can do it online. You could research that, too. What do you think? Should I drive you to the restaurant and come back to pick you up at noon?"

A familiar feeling of panic surged within her. Somehow she'd thought she'd have several days to get used to the idea before anything else new happened. Now she was supposed to spend the entire morning at the restaurant?

"It'll be just like being here." Ned stabbed a forkful of sausage. "You can go into the restaurant, lock the door and you'll be alone until I come to get you. You'll have your phone with you and there's music there. Rob got it all set up. You'll be fine."

"Okay." Might as well start now as anytime else.

Chapter Seven

A S NED UNLOCKED the door to Fila's, he glanced at the darkened building next door. It was far too early in the morning for most people to be up and about, and he wondered if Camila was still asleep, or already getting ready for her day.

Like Fila's, the windows of Camila's restaurant were papered over. She had no sign, and there was nothing to suggest that a restaurant was coming, but Ned still had an uneasy feeling when he thought about it. Camila was so outgoing and flashy. Fila was so reserved. Would Camila's restaurant overshadow Fila's place and run it right out of business? He sure as hell hoped not.

It was hard to get Camila out of his mind, though, as they entered the darkened space. Ned switched on the lights and showed Fila which toggle operated which lights, then showed her the thermostat and how to adjust it. He took her into the kitchen and showed her the iPod, too. Since Rob had already set up the online station, all they had to do was turn it on.

Ned sensed Fila relaxing as the music flowed through the speakers. She pulled her laptop out of the woven bag she carried it in and set it up on one of the tables in front. He watched helplessly as she worked out how to get connected to the Internet, and breathed a sigh of relief when the instructions Rob had left them worked like a charm. He was useless when it came to that stuff.

"Oh," Fila said, straightening suddenly. "I read through the material in the envelope you gave me yesterday. I've got it in my bag. It all seems clear. Do you want the same order as last time?"

Ned felt a rush of relief. "Yes."

"I'll take care of it."

"I appreciate it. I've got another busy day ahead of me." He stood up to leave. "Are you going to be okay? There should be plenty for you to do and research."

Fila stood up too. "I will be okay."

He hesitated. "By the way. There's a woman—her name's Camila. She's opening a restaurant next door. I thought I should warn you. She stopped by yesterday."

Fila frowned. Could she see how reluctant he was to mention her? Was she wondering why?

"I'll see you at lunch," he said, wishing he could reassure her somehow, but not knowing what to say.

"Okay."

They both hesitated. Did she want him to kiss her again?

He wished he had the guts to do so, but instead he turned and left, cursing himself all the way.

"DID THAT ORDER get done?" Luke asked when Ned found him in the barn.

"All taken care of."

"You run to Mom for help?"

"Nope." Ned loaded the cart attached to the small tractor with hay a bale at a time, stacking them up carefully so they wouldn't tip on the bumpy ride to the cattle. He refused to let Luke goad him this morning.

"You ran to someone for help."

"You through?" Ned turned on him.

"Not by a long shot. Don't know what Dad was thinking, putting you in charge. I'm the one that oughta take over for Jake."

"What makes you better than me?"

"I can do the whole job myself, for one thing."

Here they went. It all came down to reading and writing, everywhere he turned. Did Luke think it didn't burn him that he had to rely on Fila for help? That he couldn't help her set up her Internet, or research which class to take before she opened her restaurant? He was hemmed in by his lack of ability every damn day. He didn't need his little brother to pour salt in the wound.

"Take it up with Dad. I suggest you spell out exactly what your beef with me is, too. That's bound to get him on your side."

Luke turned away in disgust and Ned snorted. Yeah, he thought that's how his brother would react. Given that Holt's dyslexia was worse than his, Holt wouldn't have a lot of sympathy for Luke's feelings on the matter. Holt relied on Lisa to help him with the parts of running the ranch that required paperwork. He wouldn't have an issue with Ned using Fila.

Or maybe he would.

Ned sighed. He figured his father would come around sooner or later about Fila as long as he stuck to his guns.

Keeping the family together trumped everything in Holt's book, even if he did strut and whine and bellow when he didn't get his way. All he had to do was weather this particular storm and Holt would find something else to turn his attention to. After all, his second priority was getting his sons married and on the way to producing grandkids. Once he married Fila and they had a child, Holt would be putty in their hands.

As he trundled the load of hay out to the cattle, the problem of his dyslexia churned in his mind, though. He had a lot of years ahead of him. A lot of tasks that required reading. Using Fila to help was one way to skin that cat, but he didn't like the taste that thought left in his mouth. A man shouldn't be less than his wife; he knew that for a fact. She might not mind now. He knew Fila felt just as off-balance and uncertain in her new life as he felt when it came time to read. She'd get over that, though.

He'd never get over his dyslexia.

Despite himself, his mind leapt to the woman who'd tested him in grade school. Mrs. Martin, a gray-haired, determined woman who'd sat him down when the results came in and gave him the news in a no-nonsense manner.

"You can beat this, you know," she'd stated firmly. "It'll take work and lots of it, but there's no reason you shouldn't learn to read."

In that moment he'd believed her, but when he went home with a packet full of paperwork for his folks, and his mother had described the special tutoring sessions he'd need to attend, his father had pitched a fit.

"No son of mine is going to no *special* classes. I know what that word means and there's not a thing wrong with Ned's brain. I won't have the whole town talking about my son that way." And he'd kept on going until even his mother gave up on the project.

Ned had been secretly relieved. He knew other kids who slipped out of class when the teaching assistants came to call for them. He knew how the rest of the kids in the classroom snickered and talked behind their backs. He got enough of that already.

But looking back, Ned wondered if he'd made a mistake. Could the problem have been fixed somehow?

Was it too late?

Chapter Eight

ONCE NED WAS gone, Fila locked the door behind him and made a slow loop through the restaurant to really take it in. Without the crowd of friends in it, she noticed details she hadn't seen before—the smooth, polished tables, the geometric designs on the walls, the gleam of the counter, the beautiful frame on the chalkboard waiting for her menu.

Her friends had done their best to create something beautiful for her and it nearly moved her to tears. Just a few months ago she hadn't known any of them. Now they'd spent their free time and harnessed all their creativity to present something like this to her? She had to succeed— she couldn't let them down. She tried to imagine how it would feel to run it but found that was beyond her powers.

Returning to her laptop, she tapped her fingers while trying to decide where to start. She wasn't the whiz on a computer that all her friends seemed to be, but once she'd figured out how to use an Internet browser she'd quickly realized that research was something she thrived on. Today she decided to start with the basics. Typing *how to start a restaurant* into the search engine, she was rewarded with all kinds of sites discussing the topic. She opened a word processing program and began to build a list.

An hour and a half later, she was feeling overwhelmed, but she had managed to locate online courses for the food safety programs she needed and had a basic feel for the steps required to license her business.

Now she needed to plan a menu, so she could make a list of pots, pans, and utensils she'd need to stock her kitchen and to begin to outline an ingredients shopping plan. She knew how to plan a meal for a set number of diners, and how to plan for extras just in case, but she had no idea how to make a plan when she had no idea how many customers might come on a certain evening. What if she ran out? What if she made far too much? If she didn't do it right, she'd be wasting Ned's money, and it would take longer to earn enough to pay him back for everything he'd done.

When the knock came on the restaurant's front door, Fila nearly jumped out of her skin. She'd been so busy trying to crack the problem, she'd forgotten where she was. On the positive side, that meant she felt comfortable enough here not to have a panic attack. On the negative side, her stomach was cramping severely now to make up for that.

She approached the door with trepidation, but when she unlocked and opened it a crack, she saw a woman about her own height and size on the other side of it.

"Fila?" the woman said brightly. "I'm Camila—I'm opening a restaurant next door to yours. Can I come in?"

"Okay." Fila only hesitated a moment. Surely this slight, cheerful woman couldn't do her any harm. She held the door open and Camila walked inside.

"I love what you've done to this place. It's really gorgeous," she said. "I couldn't wait to meet you. Ned let me in last time and I met some of your other friends when they were fixing up the place for you. You're so lucky knowing so many people here. I've been here a month and I hardly know anyone."

"It's nice to meet you," Fila stammered when Camila's torrent of words came to a halt.

"Isn't opening a restaurant exciting?" Camila tossed her thick, dark hair. "I can't wait until the first night. I'm going to have a huge party. Live music and everything. These cowboys won't know what hit them!"

"That sounds nice," Fila murmured.

"Nice! It'll be better than nice! It'll be spectacular!" Camila crossed her arms in mock outrage. "What about you? What are you going to do opening night?"

"I don't know. I haven't thought that far ahead."

"Opening night is huge. Your whole success depends on it. You have to contact the local paper and radio personalities, try to get them to come so they'll promote the place for you. You should mail something out to everyone in town, put flyers on people's cars—lots of things like that. I'll help you if you like. Women should stick together, right? So—is Ned your boyfriend?"

Fila's head whirled at her sudden change in topic. "Uh...no!" Was he? She wasn't sure.

"Oh—good!" Camila grinned. "He's hot, isn't he?" She fanned herself with her hand. "I was afraid there wouldn't be anyone worth dating up here in the sticks. I didn't want to come to Montana." Her tone was confidential, leaving Fila no time to formulate the words she needed to say. "But now I see I was mistaken. The men around here are a lot more handsome than I expected. Especially Ned. He looks like he'd be all kinds of fun in the sack!"

Outrage blossomed within Fila. She pulled back. "I think I must get back to work."

Camila's expression faltered as Fila shooed her toward the door the way she'd shooed the scrawny village chickens out of her way when they congregated too close to her. "I'm sorry. I didn't—" She broke off, suddenly contrite. "Did I say the wrong thing? I didn't mean to."

"No, no," Fila said. "But I have to go."

"You'll come over and see my restaurant, won't you?" Camila walked to the door reluctantly.

"Another time." Fila knew she was being rude. She knew she would probably regret it later when she was home alone in her room, but she couldn't stand to listen to another word of Camila's banter. What right did she have to imagine Ned in bed?

None.

"Fila." Camila was truly distressed as she slipped back out the door. "Whatever I said, I didn't mean it. I hoped we'd be friends. I don't have any friends here."

"Good-bye," Fila said firmly and closed the door in her face.

FILA WAS WAITING by the door with her coat on when Ned came to fetch her for lunch. He tried to gauge her state of mind from her expression, but it was hard to read. Although she wore jeans and cowboy boots, her bearing made her outfit seem far more formal than it was.

"How did your morning go?"

"Very well," she assured him as they locked up.

"Want to go home or out to eat?"

"Home, please."

"Are you sure?"

"Ned!" Camila's bright voice broke through their discussion and Ned and Fila both turned to see her poking her head out of the door of the building next to Fila's. "Won't you come and see the place? I'd love to get your opinion on it! Hi, Fila!"

"Sure thing." Ned lowered his voice. "That's Camila—the woman I told you about." He led the way toward her. "Fila, this is Camila. Camila, this is Fila."

"We've already met, silly," Camila said, giving his arm a playful punch. "Come on in. Tell me what you think!"

Ned's stomach tightened as they entered the space. In many ways it was similar to Fila's restaurant, with a modest seating space up front, a counter splitting the building in two and behind the counter a wall cutting off the front of the restaurant from the kitchen and storage rooms. Camila had painted the upper two-thirds of her walls a vibrant chili pepper red. The lower third was black. A border of chili peppers on a black and white checked background separated the two. The tables and booths were chrome, and there was a counter along the inner wall with chrome stools in front of it. Large mirrors on the side walls created the illusion of more space. The menu on the wall behind the counter had been painted black on a white background, with more chili peppers and black and white checks forming a border around it.

"It looks great." It really did. And Mexican food was much more familiar to the inhabitants of Chance Creek than Afghan food would be. Not for the first time, he wondered if Fila's restaurant would suffer in comparison.

Camila beamed at him. "The fixtures were all here. I just had to paint. Come taste my homemade salsa." She dragged him by the hand to a booth where a red plastic basket full of chips sat on the table next to a black bowl filled with salsa. "Come on, Fila!" She waved her over as Ned took a seat and she shoved in beside him.

Ned shrugged at Fila and gestured to the opposite seat. Fila slowly sat down across from him.

She watched Camila scoop up a heaping portion of the salsa with a tortilla chip, toss her thick, dark curls over her shoulder, and feed the chip to Ned, holding her other hand cupped underneath it to catch any drips. Ned gamely allowed her to poke the chip right into his mouth. As he bit into it his face lit up.

"That's good!"

Camila's mouth stretched into a wide smile. "Do you really think so?" She leaned in toward him.

"Give me another one so I can be certain."

"Sure thing, cowboy," she said, her slight accent making the statement seem somehow provocative. She scooped up another chip full of salsa and fed it to Ned, who leaned closer to catch it in his mouth. "Go ahead, Fila," Camila said, resting a hand on Ned's bicep. "Take one. Tell me what you think."

Fila frowned, but she took one, dipped it in the salsa and took a bite. She nodded admiringly. She seemed subdued, but then Fila was always quiet around new people. Ned figured she and Camila would soon be fast friends.

"I'll make you some tostadas tomorrow," Camila promised Ned, leaning in closer and feeding him yet another chip.

"It's time for lunch," Fila said suddenly.

"What? Oh, right." Ned helped himself to a chip. He'd be fine staying right here and consuming a whole plate of them. He noticed Camila watching him, and held the chip in front of her mouth instead of eating it himself. "Your turn. Open wide."

She did so and he popped it in. Camila ate the chip, then licked the salt from her lips. "That is good, if I do say so myself."

Fila stood up suddenly, bumping the table so the salsa bowl slid several inches toward their side.

"Whoa—slow down." Ned caught it handily. "I guess we'd better get going." Fila sure seemed anxious to leave all of a sudden.

Camila took her time getting to her feet and when she did, she stretched luxuriously. Ned couldn't help notice she had a fine figure. Like Fila, she was short but curvy. Just the way he liked women. "I've been up since dawn," she said. "I'm about ready for my siesta. I don't imagine you do that around here, though, do you?"

"Unfortunately not." Ned winked at Fila. "Sounds like a good idea to me. Say, we're off to get some lunch. Want to come?"

Fila opened her mouth, then snapped it closed again. Whoops—he'd said he'd take her home, hadn't he? Well, it wouldn't kill her to eat out. A friend like Camila could be just the thing to draw her out of her shell.

"Sure!" Camila smiled broadly again. "Where are you planning to eat?"

"How about Linda's Diner? It ain't Mexican food, but it's filling."

"Let's go." Camila linked her arm with his, then turned

to Fila and hooked her other arm through hers. Fila stiffened at the contact, but didn't say anything. Good. Playful Camila would have Fila loosened up in no time. She had none of the fears Fila had, and with her obvious restaurant experience she could most likely give Fila all kinds of pointers. Maybe the proximity of the two restaurants would help, Ned thought. People liked variety. They would come to Camila's place and see Fila's on the way in. Maybe next time they'd go there.

"What brought you to Chance Creek?" he asked Camila once they were seated in a booth at the diner, looking over the menus Tracey Richards had handed them.

Camila made a face. "I'm being punished." She folded her hands and sat as primly as a schoolmarm. "I've disgraced my family so I've been sent to Siberia to learn the error of my ways."

"What was the error?"

"Being a better chef than my older brother. He's been being groomed to take over my family's restaurant in Houston for ages, but for the last year I ran the kitchen once a week—on Mondays, the slowest day for a restaurant." Camila played with her fork. "Except after a few months, Mondays became our second best sales day—better than Friday nights. Customers began to ask why the food wasn't as good on the other nights of the week. Mateo was not amused. Neither was my father."

"He didn't let you take over on the other days?" Fila spoke up for the first time.

"No. He found me a husband." Camila tossed the napkin away. "Actually brought a business associate of his home to meet me. And told me when I was married I could cook for my family. I told him no way. I left the next day."

"How did you have the money to start a restaurant?" Again, it was Fila who spoke. Ned suppressed a smile. See, friends already.

"My uncle has a slightly more forward vision of women's capabilities. He told me he'd front me the money as long as I picked a location where my father would never want to open a restaurant. So I picked Chance Creek. Even my father can't have a problem with that." Her expression conveyed that no one would want to start a restaurant here. Ned tamped down a desire to stick up for the place.

"Must be tough not to be supported by your father," he said. He could relate.

Camila shrugged. "Maybe I don't need his support."

"Maybe he'll come after you when his restaurant starts losing money." It was Fila speaking again. Ned wasn't sure he'd ever seen her so animated in company before.

"I doubt it." But Camila's mood seemed to lighten after that. "What are you getting?" She touched the back of Ned's hand where he held his laminated menu.

"A bacon burger. How about you?"

"A Cobb salad, I think. What about you, Fila?" Camila's smile was perfectly friendly, but Fila was frowning again. What was that about?

"Fila?" Ned shifted closer. "Don't you know what you want to eat yet?"

She glanced down and pointed at an item at random. "That one."

Camila craned her neck to see. "Meat loaf?"

"Are you sure?" Ned said. "How about fried chicken strips? You liked them at Autumn's house."

She flashed him a grateful smile. "Yes. Chicken strips would be good." Under the table, Ned twined his fingers briefly with hers and gave her a reassuring squeeze. She met his gaze, studied him a moment, and then relaxed.

"Hi, Ned, Fila. Didn't know we'd see you here."

Ned looked up at the sound of a familiar voice and spotted his mother's blue wool coat. Her face above it was alight in happiness at seeing him. His father, walking behind her, took in Fila next to him and Camila across the table. As he scanned Camila's vibrant features, a crafty look came into his eyes.

Before Ned could act, Holt approached the table, reached across it and offered Camila his hand. "Pleased to meet you," he said. "Holt Matheson. I'm Ned's father."

"Nice to meet you." Camila flashed him her widest smile. "I'm Camila Torres."

"Haven't seen you around here before."

"I'm new in town. Just getting to know the place."

"New in town, huh? You'll have to come and visit our ranch sometime. The Double-Bar-K is one of the oldest in the county. Any friend of Ned's is a friend of ours."

"Yes, come to Sunday dinner," Lisa chimed in. "I'm sure Fila would love to have you there."

Ned didn't miss the implications of his parents' statements. Holt was treating Camila like Ned was dating her instead of Fila. Lisa was letting him know she assumed she was Fila's friend. No good could come of the invitation either way. "I doubt Camila's interested in our ranch," he began.

Camila cut him off. "Are you kidding? All I do is hang out at the Flying W if I'm not at the restaurant, and everyone there is so busy they don't have much time for me. I'd love to see your ranch. What time?"

"Six o'clock sharp," Lisa said. "Ned will give you the

directions. We'd better go get our lunch." She poked Holt in the ribs.

"At the restaurant, huh? Are you a chef?" Holt asked, not budging.

"Yes."

"Can you make a steak?"

"Best steak you ever had. You come by my place once I'm open. I'll give you one on the house, Mr. Matheson."

"That's a deal. I'll hold you to it." He turned to Fila. "Stick with this lady. She can teach you something."

Before Ned could say a word, Lisa took hold of her husband's elbow. "Stop being cantankerous. Where's my dinner, old man?"

"Don't old man me." But Holt allowed himself to be led away. Ned breathed a sigh of relief.

"What was that all about?" Camila watched them go. "Don't you cook steaks, Fila?"

"No," Fila said shortly.

"You should taste her *bolani*," Ned put in loyally.

"I'd love to. What is it?" Camila's eyes danced with fun.

A glance told Ned Fila didn't share her amusement at the situation. "Flatbreads," he explained. "Best thing you've ever tasted. Of course, I'm biased."

Camila's gaze flicked from him to Fila and she frowned for a moment. An instant later, she tossed her lustrous hair over her shoulder and gave him another smile. "I don't think I've ever tried Afghan food before. I'm looking forward to it."

Ned couldn't help but smile back.

Chapter Nine

F ILA WAS BEGINNING to think the meal would go on forever when Camila looked at her watch and gasped. "I'm going to be late." She fished in her purse and threw a twenty dollar bill on the table, but Ned picked it up and handed it back to her.

"My treat today."

As yet another hundred-watt smile flashed across Camila's pretty face, Fila tensed.

"Thanks! I'll get it next time."

"Where are you off to in such a rush?" Ned asked.

It was like she wasn't even there, Fila thought. Of course that was her fault. If she didn't talk, why would anyone notice her?

"Volunteering! See you soon!"

Then Camila was gone in a whirlwind of coats and scarves and clicking heels. After she left, the atmosphere at their table felt dull and flat.

"Nice girl, huh?" Ned said, finishing up his lunch.

Fila nodded. Nice was hardly the word for Camila. Brilliant. Exciting. Beautiful. She was a peacock to Fila's sparrow.

"Something wrong? Should we get you home?"

She stifled a sigh. Ned was so in tune with her needs. Too bad those needs were so boring. What if they weren't, though? What if she was the kind of girl who longed to ride a horse, or learn to drive, or go to a concert—or be kissed? Would his intuition be even more keenly tuned to hers? Would he grow more interested with each passing day rather than less, as she feared he would soon do? No hot-blooded man wanted to be burdened with a timid, weepy woman like her.

So she'd have to change. Starting right now.

Right…now.

"I'd like to learn to ride a horse."

Ned nearly dropped his fork. "Are you serious?"

"Yes." She wasn't. She didn't want to be. But she had to be. And wow—was he definitely interested now. Could he read the fear in her trembling voice or had she held it steady?

"I'll teach you any time." He glanced outside at the snow that was falling and made a face. "We might have to wait a bit."

That was fine with Fila. Just the suggestion had made Ned light up. He wasn't thinking about Camila's pretty face or wide smile now, was he? That's what was important.

"I know the perfect horse, too. We'll have you riding like a pro in no time. I bet you'll end up in the rodeo."

Now it was her turn to smile, and though she knew hers wasn't nearly as bright as Camila's, nor did she laugh out loud like Camila would have done, it brought out an answering shine in Ned's eyes.

"I swear I can see it now." He nudged her gently. "Fila Sahar—star barrel racer."

"What is a barrel racer?"

"What's a barrel racer? Hell, girl. We need to get you to a rodeo!"

"HERE YOU GO, boss." Luke dropped a stack of folders on Ned's workbench late that afternoon. Outside, the sky had already darkened to dusk and more snow was falling. Flakes sparkled on Luke's wide shoulders and pooled around his feet.

"What the hell is that?"

"Taxes. The appointment with the accountant is next Tuesday. You'll want to go through all that before you hand it in to him."

Ned dropped the screwdriver he'd been using to disassemble a tow-behind trimmer and stood up. "Mom does the taxes."

"She won't last forever."

"Hell, she's only in her sixties. I don't think she'd care for you acting like she's on death's door."

"I don't think she should have to handle the paperwork at her age."

Ned moved away from the workbench. "So I bet you told her you'd do it, then you dumped the job in my lap. You can just take it back again."

Luke squared off with him. "I think whoever is in charge oughta know how to keep the books."

"What the hell is this really about?" As if he didn't know.

"It ain't fair—that's what this is about. Just because you were born a year ahead of me don't mean you know anything I don't know. I can run this place—I know it! I just want a chance."

"And you figured this is the way you'd go about getting that chance? By making me look like an idiot? Grow up, Luke."

"Grow up? Damn it—that's what everyone says. What I want to know is how the hell can I grow up if no one is ever going to give me any responsibility?"

Ned heard the note of desperation in his brother's voice and had a flash of insight. "This isn't about the ranch at all, is it? This is about Mia."

"No, it ain't."

"Yes, it is. She's the one telling you to grow up, isn't she? Why? What did you do to her?"

Luke lifted his hands up in air. "I didn't do anything! She's been acting weird for weeks. Friendly one minute, cold as ice the next. It's your fault, too—it's that baby thing."

"Baby thing?"

"Mia was fine until you spilled the beans about Hannah being pregnant—back when we thought she was pregnant. That's when Mia got all crazy."

Ned thought back to when all three women had moved onto the ranch. Hannah and Jake had had an incident with their birth control and thought there was a chance Hannah had gotten pregnant. Since Hannah had just decided to go back to school, the news caused an uproar—an uproar he'd made use of to try to unseat Jake from heading up the ranch, in the same way Luke was trying to unseat him now. Ned grimaced at the irony, but what could you expect with his family? They were always at loggerheads for this exact reason—all of them wanted to be in charge.

"You're blaming me because Mia got upset about Hannah being pregnant?"

"I'm blaming you because if you hadn't announced it, I wouldn't have said—" Luke shoved his hands in his pockets and turned away.

"What did you say?" Something stupid, by the look on his brother's face.

"When it looked like it wasn't going to be true after all, I said, 'No baby, no problem.'"

Ned chuckled. "Hell, you dug your own damn hole, then. Even I know better than to say something like that."

"She's held it against me ever since. I just said it—I didn't mean anything by it."

"But let me guess. Mia wants kids and now she thinks you don't."

Luke looked surprised. "How did you know that?"

"I'm not the idiot here."

Luke let that go. "Now she won't even date me. She won't even let me touch her."

No wonder why Luke was so cranky these days. "So tell her you want kids."

"Just how in the hell am I supposed to start that conversation?" Color crept up Luke's face and he kicked a can of paint sitting on the floor.

"Watch it." Ned thought a minute. "That happened weeks ago and Mia is still living with you. If you'd screwed things up for good, she wouldn't have stuck around this long. She must want to be with you. You just gotta get past this."

"How?"

"You know people with kids. Talk to them. Play ball with them. Hold a baby. Mia will get the picture. And then talk to her, too. Even if it's hard."

"You think that will work?"

"I don't see why not."

After a moment, Luke nodded. "All right. I'll do it." Now he seemed as eager to leave as Ned was to have him go. He hesitated, then picked up the folders he dropped on the workbench earlier. "I'll take care of this, too."

Ned was relieved he'd taken the tax documents with him, but he hated the knowledge that here was another task related to the ranch that he couldn't handle on his own.

The thought of approaching someone for help learning to read after all this time filled him with dread.

The alternative seemed little better.

"YOU WORK FAST," Mia said several days later, studying the menu Fila had written up for her restaurant on her laptop.

"What do you think about it?" They were seated at the table in Mia and Luke's cabin. Fila had to hide a smile every time she came over. As soon as she'd moved in, Mia had redecorated the place in bright pink. Everyone laughed when they saw it, but Mia didn't seem to care. She simply declared her undying love for the color and told people if they didn't like it they could leave.

No one did.

Like Camila, Mia was one of those women who seemed supremely self-possessed. Her tiny size, fashion sense and waist-length ponytail all combined to make her look like a wayward teenager, and her bubbly personality and ringing laugh turned heads wherever she went.

Why couldn't she be like that, Fila wondered for the hundredth time. Mia was right—she should run the front of the restaurant. She'd be far better at dealing with customers than Fila ever would.

"I don't know what all these dishes are. You need descriptions for each one. If you tell me about them I can help you write them up." She wrinkled her nose. "That's a spelling error. And here's another one." She went through the document and made corrections.

"I'm bad at spelling."

"Well I'm not blaming you, I'm not much better," Mia laughed. "How were you supposed to learn living in those mountains? I had a hard enough time here in the good ol' U.S. of A. Do you need any help with the food safety course?"

Fila had filled her in on the online course she was taking. "I don't think so. I don't think spelling counts." *Thank goodness.* Her spelling wasn't quite on par with her reading ability. "The materials were easy enough."

"Good. What about a business plan? Are you going to make one of those?" At Fila's blank look, Mia pulled up a search engine and typed in some words. "Here's one— look." She showed Fila a long document that asked many questions about the business one was trying to run, in order to find out whether or not it was likely to succeed.

Fila quickly became overwhelmed as she tried to read through it. "I don't even know what half of these terms mean. What's a benchmark?"

"I think it's a fancy way of saying *goal.*"

"Then they should just say goal."

Mia chuckled. "We could do it together. I'd really like to. My job is so boring. It's just the same thing every day. I know I can do more than that—so you'd be helping me as much as I'd be helping you. You know I'm dying to work with you so I can quit the hardware store. Together we can make sure we do this right so the restaurant succeeds, you know?"

At Fila's questioning look, Mia went on. "Look, I don't make a lot of money at Dundy's. I'm kind of stuck. I can afford to live with Luke because the rent is so cheap, but if I have to leave I don't know what I'm going to do."

"You and Luke aren't getting along?"

Mia sighed. "I don't know. Sometimes I think we'd make a great couple. Other times—he's such a man!"

"He likes you."

"I know." But Mia didn't look happy. "I have to be sure of him before I make up my mind. I can't make any mistakes."

Fila wasn't sure she understood. American women seemed to have no trouble dating a few men before settling down with one. Why would Mia be any different?

"Anyway, my love life doesn't matter." Mia pushed her ponytail over her shoulder and hunched over the laptop again. "Should we work on your menu or on the business plan?"

Chapter Ten

NED COULDN'T REMEMBER the last time he'd sidled into his mother's kitchen with so much trepidation. Probably not since the time he'd been busted at sixteen for stealing the high school principal's car and doing donuts in the Wright's hayfield with it. He'd settled down a lot since those days, and he figured this errand would please his mother, but he hated the thought of the fuss she'd make just as much as he'd dreaded her reaction back then.

"Ned. What are you doing here this time of day? Everything all right?" His mother was bent over one of the cookbooks his grandmother had passed down to her. She pushed it aside and gestured to another chair at the kitchen table.

"Everything's fine. Just had a question."

"Want some tea? I was just about to pour myself some." She got to her feet and bustled about the kitchen in her usual fashion.

"Juice is good." Ned didn't bother to try to get it himself. She'd just wave him back into his seat. His mother had always liked to take care of her family and he got the feeling sometimes she still saw him and his brothers as the little boys they once were. She'd be in heaven once she had some grandkids.

"What's the question?"

He waited until she was sitting down again. "If I wanted to—" Now that it was time to ask, he didn't know what words to use. His mother waited patiently. "If I wanted to try it again. Reading. What would I do?"

"Ah." Lisa sat back and nodded, her hands cupped around her steaming mug of tea. She didn't seem surprised by his sudden question. Had she anticipated it now that he'd taken over managing the herd? "Given you're past school age, I think you'd need to find a literacy tutor."

"Where would I get one of those?"

Lisa thought a moment. "I think I might know. Mind if I make a phone call?"

"Have at it." Now that it was out in the open, he just wanted things sorted as fast as possible. Lisa stepped away and made a call after looking up a number. He heard her describing what she wanted—someone to meet with him one on one to work on his reading skills—and after a few moments jotted something down on a piece of paper. Five minutes later she was back in her seat pushing the paper across the table at him. "Go to 5454 Third Street. Second floor. Room eight. Monday at two o'clock."

"What is it?"

"A volunteer bureau. They'll assign a literacy tutor to you. The program is free, so you won't see a specialist, exactly—just someone trained to work with people with dyslexia. I imagine you'll go once a week and they'll give you homework in between." She must have seen his expression. "Ned, you and your father like to act like you're the only ones with this problem, but you're not. It's so common you can't throw a stone in a crowded room without hitting someone with dyslexia. I know they can help. I'm glad you're going to give it a try."

"Don't tell Dad." He stood up and shoved the scrap of paper into his pocket.

"I won't tell him. But if he does find out somehow, you don't listen to what he says. You can do this. It kills me I let him talk me out of getting you help years ago." She shook her head. "Sometimes I think I must be the worst mother in the world."

Ned snorted. "You're the best and you know it. You're just fishing for compliments."

She gave him a wry smile. "Not in this case. In this case I think I did you a disservice. I hope you can forgive me."

He nodded. "Of course. I know why you didn't push."

"That doesn't make what I did right."

He dropped a kiss on her head. "You get to be human, too, Mom. What's done is done."

"Get yourself to that appointment and undo it, you hear?"

"Yes, ma'am."

WHEN FILA ENTERED the Cruz Big House with Ned later that night, most of the pool and poker players had already arrived. As usual, her stomach filled with butterflies as she geared up to walk into the crowded living room, but shedding her coat and entering the fray wasn't nearly as difficult as it normally was. She carried a basket of *bichak*— a kind of pastry with a cheese filling—for everyone to try. She was considering them as an appetizer on her menu, but wasn't sure if they'd be popular. She figured she would simply set them down on the counter between the living room and kitchen. If they were gone by the time they went home, she'd add them to the menu.

In the end, they were gone before anyone even sat down to play cards, and Fila had to endure a throng of enthusiastic eaters thanking her for bringing them along and pressing her for more. She bore up under the friendly assault, however. With Ned standing quietly at her back, she found she could handle the attention. When it began to overwhelm her, Ned said loudly, "When are we going to get started? I plan to take home some cash tonight!"

That diverted everyone's attention and the players soon settled down at several tables Autumn and Ethan had set up for just this purpose. As people were knocked out of the Hold'em game, they generally wandered over to the pool table to try their hand at that.

Usually Fila sat on the outskirts or busied herself in the kitchen during the games, but today Ned caught her hand and tugged her to the table. "I'm going to teach you how it's played tonight." He wouldn't listen to her protests and soon she found herself seated between him and Morgan.

When Ethan dealt the cards for their table, Ned told him they'd share a hand. "It'll take you a bit to get the hang of it, so for now you watch," he told Fila. As he walked her through the game, at first she could barely concentrate on his words. She was too aware of the others at the table—too aware of the men mixed in with the women, something that seldom happened in the village back in Afghanistan. She found herself plucking at a burka that wasn't there, wanting to hide her face.

"Hey. No one's going to hurt you here," Ned said in a low voice. "Look at the cards, not at the crowd."

She did as he said and he started his explanation over. After a few minutes, she got caught up in the game. She watched what Ned did and noticed how the other players reacted. Several minutes later, when it was Ned's turn to make a move, she pointed to the card she wanted him to discard and he nodded. "Now you're getting it."

His praise brought a smile to her face. She caught Morgan's eye and Morgan smiled back, her dark hair loose around her shoulders. "Fun, isn't it? Just wait until you start betting."

The pile of dollar bills in front of Ned was growing, much to her satisfaction.

"Fila must be your lucky charm," Jake said in disgust the next time Ned raked in the pot.

"Lucky, nothing. She's whispering what to do in my ear." Ned pulled in all the dollar bills and stacked them neatly to the side.

"She can come here and whisper in my ear, then," Jake said.

"She'd better not," Hannah called out from the other table.

As the room erupted in laughter, Fila felt her cheeks warm. Her hands curled around the arms of the chair she sat in.

Ned covered one of them with his. "Don't mind them. They wouldn't joke with you like that if they didn't like you. You know that, right?"

She nodded and took deep breaths like Autumn had taught her. In and out. In and out.

"Tell me what to do now," Ned said, holding the cards where she could see them. She bent closer, considering, and didn't even notice when her panic slid away.

"Fila, are you sure you don't have any more of those appetizer things with you?" Rose called out some minutes later. The petite brunette sat next to Cab, who towered over everyone else in the room. Fila had been intimidated by the large sheriff until she got to know him.

Fila shook her head. "Sorry."

"Bring more next time," Jamie Lassiter said.

"Yeah!" Several voices chimed in.

"I know what you should do," Mia said brightly. "You should have a big taste testing party. You could make up a bunch of things you plan to put on the menu at your restaurant and everyone could have a little bit of everything. Then people could vote on them. The most popular dishes would win."

"That's a great idea," Cab called out. Everyone laughed.

"It is a good idea, though. You could use my kitchen— I'd be glad to host the party here," Autumn said.

"I think she should have it at the restaurant," Rose said. "That way she'd get a chance to try all the appliances out and make sure they work right. It would be a test run for the place."

"I want to test run taking orders and working the register!" Mia said, nearly bouncing in her chair.

"What do you think?" Ned asked her. "A week from Saturday, maybe?"

After a moment's hesitation, Fila nodded slowly. "Okay," she said.

Her anxiety came rushing back.

Chapter Eleven

NED HAD LIVED in Chance Creek all his life, so it surprised him to realize he'd never noticed 5454 Third Street before. It was a nondescript two story building containing a chiropractor's office, a cleaning business and the Chance Creek Volunteer Center on the second floor. When he opened the door to the center, he found himself in a reception area with a no-nonsense gray carpet and black and gray metal chairs set up in a waiting area. He introduced himself to a middle-aged woman behind the counter and she told him to take a seat.

He did so, noting the battered toys in a basket in one corner and dog-eared magazines on the end tables. Apparently, not everyone who came here was illiterate.

"Ned? Is that you?"

At the sound of his name, dread tightened his chest. Damn—he'd been found out. As his mind raced to concoct a reason why he'd be in such a place, he scanned the room for the speaker. He knew that bright, cheerful voice, even if he couldn't place it immediately. He caught sight of Camila standing at the edge of the waiting area. Today she wore a knee-length red pencil skirt, a black blouse and red baubles at her throat and wrists. The large, chunky jewelry would have looked ridiculous on anyone else. On Camila, they looked just fine.

"What are you doing here?" His response was far gruffer than he'd intended and for a moment she looked taken aback.

"I'm your tutor! Isn't that a coincidence? I nearly freaked out when I saw your name on my list this morning. Come on back."

Ned stayed in his seat. He had no idea how to extricate himself from this situation. There was no way he'd let this woman tutor him. He couldn't even stand that she knew he had a problem to begin with. But could he leave without speaking to her—without an explanation? Somehow he doubted it.

"I—" He stood up and edged toward the door. "I just remembered—I mean, I can't—"

"Oh, for God's sake, get over here," Camila said impatiently. "You aren't the first man with dyslexia. Cowboy up—isn't that the phrase? Let me do my job and feel good about myself." She tapped over to him on her high heels, grabbed his sleeve and dragged him down a short hall to a small, windowless office. Inside was a table and two chairs—and little else except for a small bookcase filled with books.

Ned hovered near the door. "I don't really need—"

"Sit down and shut up, Ned. You want to learn to read and I'm going to help you. I won't tell anyone what we're doing here and by the time we're through, you'll read just as well as anyone else. Got it?"

"You've done this before?" He still sounded surly. He didn't care—he was surly.

"I have. Back in Houston." She turned serious. "Tutoring does work, Ned. People have been studying dyslexia for years. Not everyone with dyslexia will be able to read perfectly, but a lot of people can be helped by this method. Give it a chance, at least."

"How many times do I have to come here?"

"As many as it takes," she said pertly. "Commit to ten lessons, at least, okay? Just to see the difference it makes? After that you won't need any convincing."

Ned scratched the back of his neck. He wanted to turn on his heel and walk right back out of this building, but that wouldn't solve anything. He still wouldn't be able to read and Camila would still know about his dyslexia. "Okay," he said grudgingly.

"Okay, you'll stay?"

"Yeah, I'll stay."

Camila beamed at him. "It'll be great!"

"Don't push your luck."

WHEN NED HARDLY spoke at dinner time, Fila thought at first he'd had another run in with his father or brother, but when they'd cleaned up and he moved to the living room to sit on the couch, she asked if everything was okay and he nodded yes.

"Just a headache. Let's watch TV."

He clicked through the channels until he found a nature show, then leaned back against the back of the couch and shut his eyes. Fila, just coming in from the kitchen, frowned. She tentatively laid her hand on his forehead. He didn't have a fever.

"That feels good."

Fila stilled at his words, but didn't withdraw her hand. Instead, she lightly smoothed his hair back from his forehead, the way she had done to small children in the village when she was helping the healer. Ned sighed contentedly and after a moment she did it again. She liked the feel of his smooth forehead and thick hair against her fingers. When Ned murmured appreciatively, she shifted her stance and began to rub his temples. A little boy in the village—Sabir—used to get horrible headaches. One of the other women told her he'd seen his parents killed in a raid by a hostile clan. After that, she'd felt a kinship to him, and tried to be the one to soothe him when his headaches came.

She didn't realize she'd been humming as well as ministering to Ned until he opened one eye. "What's that tune?"

Fila dropped her hands and stepped back, and he groaned. "Don't stop. You don't have to tell me if you don't want."

She resumed what she was doing and searched for a way to translate the song's name. Gave up. "It's a lullaby," she explained. "Allaho sha Allaho."

Ned grunted and closed his eyes again. She kept rubbing and after a time started humming again, just under her breath. Long after Ned's breathing evened out, she kept at it. Touching him, even in this gentle way, stirred something within her that was close to longing. She'd never gotten the chance to inspect him so closely—the way his brows etched two strong blond lines across his forehead, the rise of his skin over his cheekbones, his square jaw. After a time, she stepped away from him, aware that if she kept going she was bound to wake him again and he seemed to need his sleep. She wondered what had happened this afternoon to cause his headache. She hoped he'd be better soon.

Making her way on quiet feet, she sat down carefully next to him on the couch and watched the program for a few minutes before turning to gaze at him again. Still fast asleep, Ned looked younger than he usually did. More gentle.

She knew how gentle he could be when he was awake, though, so that was no revelation. What was a revelation was how masculine he still was. She placed her hand next to his where it lay on the couch cushion and marveled at how much longer his fingers were—how his wrist was nearly twice as thick as hers. He was a powerful man.

A good man.

She turned back to the show for a few more minutes, but realized she had no idea what it was about. A man was stalking a cheetah but every time he got close, the predator raced away. After a third shot of the cheetah dashing across a savannah, Fila edged closer to Ned. He didn't wake, so she moved closer still, until her arm brushed his.

He shifted then and she froze as he lifted his arm around her shoulders and pulled her in. He didn't open his eyes and his breathing didn't shift either. If she tried to break loose, she'd awaken him for sure. Fila didn't know what to do.

As the minutes ticked past, she decided she didn't need to do anything. She leaned against his chest and was rewarded when his arm encircled her more snugly. His embrace wasn't tight enough to set her alarm bells off—on the contrary, she felt safe with Ned. She leaned her head against his shoulder, closed her eyes.

And eventually fell asleep.

Chapter Twelve

HIS ARM HAD been asleep for hours and Ned was wondering if was possible to do permanent damage to a limb this way when Fila finally stirred and woke. He wasn't complaining, though. When he'd woken an hour or two after conking out on the couch to find Fila dozing in his arms, he'd felt like Christmas had come early. She was tucked against his shoulder, her dark hair coming loose from its usual braid and tickling his nose. He had debated whether to find a blanket to cover her up, but in the end decided to stay right where he was for as long as this lasted. He'd alternately dozed and woken all night, but it was worth it. If Fila trusted him enough to snuggle with him, they were making progress fast.

"Morning, sleepyhead."

She sat up and stretched, the motion pulling her shirt tight against her breasts. Ned felt a stirring he needed to control—pronto. With an effort he did.

"Is it morning?"

"It's early. You should go up to bed and get some more sleep."

"What about you?"

For one golden second he thought she was asking him to go with her. Then his sleep-deprived brain made an effort and worked out her true meaning. "No sense my going back to bed when I have to get back up in a half-hour."

"Sorry."

He took her hand. "There's nothing for you to be sorry for. I was right where I wanted to be."

A beautiful blush stole across her skin and Ned couldn't help himself. He leaned forward and kissed her. Just a light brush of his lips over her cheek, but enough to make that color inch higher.

"Ned."

"What?" He liked seeing her like this, all sleep-tousled and rosy.

"You shouldn't do that." But she didn't seem unhappy that he had.

"I think I should." He did it again. "Come here. Might as well make the best of that half-hour." He leaned forward and grabbed a throw blanket off the back of one of the easy chairs, tugged her back against his chest and covered both of them. "Go to sleep."

"Are you sure?"

"I'm sure," he said.

But neither of them slept.

WHEN MIA CAME over mid-morning for another business plan session, she dropped her purse on the kitchen counter, peered at Fila's face and said, "What happened to you?"

"I didn't sleep well." Fila busied herself putting on a kettle for tea.

"Nightmares again?"

"No." Fila shrugged and hoped Mia wouldn't push for details. Now that she looked at her, Mia didn't look so hot herself. "Are you okay?"

"Not really." To Fila's surprise the young woman began to cry.

Comforting other people wasn't Fila's strong point—unless they were babies. There had been little tenderness between her and the other women of her village. Most of them couldn't afford to take the risk of being seen to favor her. She was too different—too apt to make the kind of mistake that brought about the wrath of the Taliban men who called the shots. So she never knew quite what to do when a situation like this presented itself, and now she hovered over Mia for a few moments before tentatively placing a hand on her arm. "What's the matter?"

"Everything! Luke. He's such an idiot!"

Fila had noticed a tension between Luke and Mia for weeks. Like Fila, Mia had moved onto the Double-Bar-K just before the beginning of December and though she'd first lived with Ned, that hadn't worked out and she'd eventually switched places with Fila to move in with Luke. Fila had expected a romance to blossom between the two almost instantly, judging by the way Luke's gaze never swerved from Mia whenever they were together.

But that hadn't happened, and she wasn't sure what the nature of the relationship between the two was. Sometimes they chatted and laughed and shot glances at each other so loaded with intent and desire Fila felt uncomfortable in their presence. Other times they moved stiffly around each other as if they had never even met. Fila couldn't fathom what was going on.

"What did he do?"

"Nothing! He's done nothing and it's almost too late!"

"Too late for what?"

Mia sobbed louder. "I've made such a stupid mistake. Such a stupid, stupid mistake. I don't know what to do! I'm going to lose him!"

"Lose Luke?" How could she lose a man who followed her around like a puppy on a string most of the time? "You're wrong. Luke worships you."

Mia dropped her hands and stared at Fila. "Now, maybe. He won't next month."

Fila chuckled despite her concern. "What do you plan to do next month? Set his cabin on fire?"

"It's not what I plan to do. It's what I've already done." Mia wiped her eyes. Fila didn't like the hopelessness in her tone. "Can you keep a secret?"

Fila nodded. She was good at that.

"I'm pregnant. And I've never been with Luke."

Understanding flooded Fila, along with a wash of fear that had her gripping the table for support. An unwed mother. What would happen? What would they do to her? Would they—

No. She wasn't in Afghanistan.

"Fila?" The concern was all too evident in Mia's voice.

Fila struggled to get a hold of herself, taking calming breaths, holding the table tight until her knuckles went white. "Sorry," she gasped out. "It'll pass."

Mia bit her lip, studying her. "What would they have done to me where you were? Would they have killed me?"

Fila shut her eyes. Possibly.

A tear slid down Mia's face. "Sometimes I think everyone would be better off if I was dead."

Fila was on her knees in an instant, her arms around Mia—all her own fears forgotten. "No! Never say that. You are a mother now. Soon you will hold your baby in your arms."

"I know," Mia wailed. "And I can't wait. I want to see my baby so badly, but don't you see—the minute Luke finds out about it, he's going to hate me."

Fila pulled back. Thought that through. Luke was proud—the proudest of the Mathesons, and that was saying a lot. You could tease Jake and Rob. Even Ned had a sense of humor, buried as it was under his gruff exterior. Luke saw things in black and white, right or wrong. He reminded her of the Taliban men that way. He honestly cared for Mia—anyone could see that—but what would he do if he knew she carried another man's child?

He would leave her. It was that simple.

Should she lie to Mia? Pretend it wasn't so? That would comfort her more than the truth. But one look at Mia's face told her it was too late for lies.

"I'm sorry," Fila said.

"It's hopeless, isn't it?" Tears streaked down Mia's cheeks. "I keep trying to figure out what to do. I hoped he'd fall so in love with me that it wouldn't matter. But it does. It will. I have to give him up."

"What will you do?"

"Work for you, I hope. Get an apartment. Do my best for my child. I got myself into this—it's up to me to figure a way through. I won't be the first single mother." But her sigh told Fila that being a single mother was the last thing Mia wanted to be.

"I will help you all I can. I love babies."

"What will I do after it's born, though? How do I pay

for child care while I work and still have enough to live on?"

"Child care?" Fila reared back, affronted at the thought. "Why would you pay for child care?"

"I can't keep a baby in the restaurant."

Fila rolled her eyes. Silly Americans. "Why not?"

Chapter Thirteen

"IT'S SO NICE of you to invite me to your family dinner," Camila exclaimed as Ned helped her off with her coat. They stood in the foyer of his parents' house on Sunday evening while the rest of the family took their places at the large dining room table.

"Fila will be glad you did," he said. "I've got to warn you, though. My family can be a bit... overwhelming."

"I have five brothers and two sisters. Don't tell me about overwhelming."

Ned led the way into the dining room where the table was set for eleven. Holt already sat in his seat at one end of the table. To his right sat Jake, Hannah, Luke and Mia. To his left, Rob and Morgan were in their chairs. Fila was helping his mother in the kitchen.

"Take your pick. My Mom usually takes the end." Ned indicated the remaining empty chairs and waited until Camila selected the middle one. He helped push her in and took the seat between her and Morgan.

"Welcome to our home," Holt said to Camila. Ned exchanged a look with Jake, who raised an eyebrow. Ned couldn't convey in a glance the reason for Holt's sudden burst of manners, but he knew the cause well enough. His father was going to use Camila to force Fila out of the picture if he didn't watch out.

"Thank you." Camila beamed at him.

"Hope you're hungry." Lisa walked into the room bearing a huge platter of ham. Fila followed with a basket of biscuits in one hand and a bowl of green beans in the other. She noticed her empty seat down at the far end of the row and made a face. Ned frowned. There wasn't much he could do about the seating arrangement now. He would have thought she'd be happy to sit next to Camila, though.

For a few minutes there was a flurry of dishes coming in from the kitchen and the passing of food around the table. When Fila finally took her place she unfolded her napkin, draped it across her lap and sat in silence, only moving to help herself to small portions of the food.

Ned sighed. She must still feel uncomfortable among all of the people here, and why wouldn't she when his father took every chance to hint that she should leave. He was determined that would change—and soon.

"Camila, tell us about yourself. What brings you to Chance Creek?" Holt cut into his slice of ham.

"I'm opening a restaurant right next door to—"

Ned coughed and cut across her words. "It's on First Street. Around the corner from DelMonaco's." He turned to Camila, caught her eye and shook his head slightly, hoping she'd understand not to bring up Fila's restaurant. So far no one had mentioned it to Holt and he meant to keep it that way until it was a done deal. Holt would have a field day if he knew Ned had financed the place.

"What kind of food? I hope not more of that foreign stuff like that one makes." Holt jabbed a finger at Fila.

"Holt!" Lisa turned to Camila, her usually kind face pinched in vexation. "Excuse him, please. His mother dropped him on his head several times when he was a baby. Unfortunately she didn't tell me about it until after we were married."

Holt stabbed a forkful of ham and chewed it vigorously.

"Well," Camila began uncertainly. "It's a Mexican food restaurant. Tacos, burritos—that kind of thing?" The normally outspoken young woman seemed cowed for the first time since Ned had met her. Holt had that effect on people, though.

"I love Mexican food—it's practically American, isn't it?" Holt stabbed another bite. All around the table, his children reared back in surprise.

"Since when do you love Mexican food?" Luke asked loudly. Mia nudged him. "What?"

"Since forever." Holt fixed him with a glare.

"I wish you would tell Mom. I wouldn't mind some tacos now and then."

"We'll have tacos next Sunday, then," Lisa said easily, but she glanced at Ned and rolled her eyes. Ned knew why—if she'd ever served tacos before, there would have been hell to pay about that *south of the border* food.

"Oh—I'll bring tacos if you like!" Camila perked up, then blushed. "I mean—I didn't mean to invite myself over again. Sorry."

"Not at all," Holt said magnanimously. "Come on over next week, too. Bring your tacos. It'll be a treat."

Lisa dropped her utensils and coughed so hard into her napkin that everyone looked her way. "That's a terrific idea," she choked out. She dabbed at her face, recovered her composure and smiled wickedly. "I'll make a big old salad to go with them." Ned laughed out loud. Holt hated salad almost as much as he hated Mexican food.

"I'll bring that dessert I make," Morgan put in smoothly. "The one with all the bananas."

Mia spit out the sip of milk she'd just taken and coughed until Luke pounded her on the back. "Sorry." She mopped herself up with her napkin. "Breathed in the wrong way."

Ned bit back the urge to laugh again. He'd forgotten how much his father hated Morgan's banana dessert. And let her know in no uncertain terms the one time she'd served it to him.

Holt's expression was getting grimmer and grimmer. From the way Camila was sneaking looks his way he figured she knew something was up, but wasn't sure what it was.

"I'll bring Nawabi Kandahari Gosht," Fila announced loudly and clearly, her voice slipping into an accent in a way he hadn't heard since her first days in town. It took him a moment to realize she'd gotten all the jokes and was adding her own jab at the old man.

"That all sounds lovely," Lisa said, smoothly preventing an outburst from Holt. "But today I hope you'll make do with my plain American fare. When did you arrive in Chance Creek, Camila?"

"Last month. I hope to open my restaurant near the first of February."

"Do you have family in town?"

"No." Camila's good humor slipped again. "It's just me. I'm staying out at the Flying W. They had a private room to rent. I don't see the owners much though. They always seem to be busy."

"The Turners? They're recovering from a bad year, I've heard. That must be lonely for you." Lisa's voice was kind.

"It is," Camila said softly. "So I'm doing my best to meet people. I hope that once I open my restaurant I'll feel like part of the community."

"That can take time," Morgan said, "but it does happen. I moved here from Canada last fall and now it really does feel like home."

"Thank you," Camila said. "Thank all of you for including me today. It means a lot to me."

"You'll always be welcome here." Holt's tone made it clear not everyone was.

Ned gripped his fork harder, knowing what his father was trying to say. Camila was welcome. Fila wasn't. He couldn't decide if his father's earlier explanation was true. Did he really think Fila was too scarred to ever heal from her experience in Afghanistan? Or was this prejudice through and through? Either way, it didn't matter. He wouldn't change his mind about Fila.

And he wasn't going to hide his feelings, either.

He reached over across Camila and covered Fila's hand with his for a moment. "You'll always be welcome here, too."

Fila smiled back at him. Camila's eyes widened. Ned patted Fila's hand and let go, turning just in time to see Holt's thunderous expression.

"I meant what I said to you." Holt pointed his knife at him.

"I meant what I said, too."

"Holt, we have company." Lisa's tone brooked no nonsense.

"That's never stopped him before," Luke said.

"Don't you cross me." Holt raised his voice, ignoring the others.

"Don't you cross me." Ned leaned forward.

"Fila—don't you think we should celebrate our grand openings together?" Camila blurted.

The table fell silent. Holt's gaze shifted to the newcomer. "What do you mean, grand openings? I thought you were the one with the restaurant."

Color stained Camila's cheeks. "Shoot! I mean... I think... I—" She trailed off unhappily.

"I have a restaurant, too," Fila said suddenly.

"You have a restaurant?" Holt turned to her. "Since when?"

Ned jumped in to rescue her. "Since just this week. Right next to Camila's on First Street."

"And how the hell is she paying for that?"

You could have heard a pin drop. All eyes turned to Ned. "I'm financing it."

"That sounds wonderful," Lisa said, beaming at him. "Two new restaurants in town. The place is shaping up."

Holt didn't even miss a beat. "You and me are going to have a little talk in the morning. Got it?"

"Got it."

The rest of the meal was a mighty quiet affair.

"THAT WENT BETTER than I expected," Mia whispered to Fila when everyone had congregated in the front hall to leave. "What was all that about Holt liking Mexican food?"

"It was about me. He wants me to leave." Fila tried not to let that get to her, but it did.

"He's such a pain in the ass. Ignore him." Mia linked her arm through hers. "Let's wait for Ned and Luke outside. I've had enough of the Mathesons as a family for one night." She pulled Fila through the throng, only pausing to hug Lisa and thank her for dinner.

Lisa patted Fila's hand. "Under all Holt's baloney, there's a man who loves his family," she said quietly. "Give him a chance and he'll come around. When he does, he'll be your biggest ally—you'll see."

Fila shrugged and thanked her for the meal, but she was relieved when they made it outside. Holt wasn't going to come around. She was sure of that. She just wasn't sure what that meant for her future. She trailed after Mia into the sharp chill of the January evening and they walked slowly together down the steps and toward the dirt road that led to the cabins, expecting the men to catch up with them at any time.

"What's taking them so long?" Mia said finally, looking over her shoulder. "Oh."

At the tone of her voice, Fila turned to look too. Ned and Camila were standing by Camila's car, talking earnestly. They stood close enough together that their low tones didn't carry to Fila's ears. After a brief discussion, Camila laughed, the sound pealing out. "See you on Monday," she said quite clearly. She leaned in and hugged Ned, then got in her car and pulled away. Ned stood watching her until her taillights disappeared before he turned and caught Fila and Mia waiting for him.

"Just making sure she remembered the way home," he said when he caught up with them.

"What are you two doing on Monday?" Fila couldn't believe she was asking, but she had to know. Ned and

Camila had acted so familiar with each other. She couldn't forget Camila's hug.

"Nothing." Ned's answer was as sharp as Holt's had been a half-hour ago. Fila pulled back, just as Luke pounded down the steps from the main house and loped their way.

"Sorry—Dad had some last minute orders for me."

Ned turned on his heel and led the way toward the cabins. Neither Fila nor Mia said a word. After a moment, Luke filled in the uncomfortable silence.

"That Camila's sure a live wire, isn't she? Getting Dad to say he liked Mexican food? He wouldn't have said that to anyone else. Guess he's not immune to a pretty face, huh?"

"Shut up, Luke." Ned picked up the pace.

"What'd I say? It's true and you know it. Dad wouldn't be caught dead eating that stuff. I love it, though. As far as I'm concerned, Camila can come by any time."

Mia huffed out a breath and stalked off toward Luke's place.

"Hey—Mia! Wait up! What's wrong?"

"Unbelievable," Ned said to Fila when they were gone. "He gets it wrong every time."

You're no better, Fila wanted to say, but she kept her mouth shut. How could she blame him for preferring Camila's company when she was so mousy and boring? Camila looked like a movie star compared to her. She was always talking and laughing. Always so full of fun. Beside her, Fila felt about as interesting as a stone. If he had been alone with Camila, what would Ned have done when he said good-bye? Would he have kissed her?

She felt certain he would.

But if they were getting together on Monday, he didn't have to risk it when all of his family was here to see. He and Camila would have as much time and privacy they wanted to kiss then.

Fila picked up her pace, too. She was all too ready to call it a night.

Chapter Fourteen

"WHEN'S THE LAST time this happened?" Rob said as he came through the barn door, stamping the snow off of his boots.

Ned looked up from retying his own boots and saw what he meant—all three of his brothers were in the barn at the same time he was. Since Jake and Rob had split off from the family, taking on their own acreages and getting busy with their own plans, it wasn't often that they worked all together.

"It's the first time I can remember standing here with all of you and not wanting to take a swing at someone," Jake said, chuckling. "I guess this new way of doing things isn't all that bad."

"I could still be persuaded to take a swing at someone," Luke said, shooting Ned a look.

"That's because Dad's still got the two of you set against each other." Rob shook his head. "It seems like this family won't ever learn. You should see how we do things at the Cruz ranch—there isn't any brawling there."

"You choose your friends," Luke said. "You don't get to choose your family."

"You can choose how you behave toward your family." Jake turned to Ned. "How's it going, being in charge?"

"Not that much to be in charge of right now. Wait until things liven up again in the spring."

Luke snorted. "If you can hold on to the job that long."

"Well, look at this. The whole gang's here." Holt let himself into the barn and shut the door against the cold wind blowing outside. "Hate to bust up the tea party, but those cattle are getting hungry."

"I'll get right on it," Ned said, pulling his gloves on.

"Hold up. I want a word with you. No, the rest of you stay put—you can all hear this."

Now what? Ned wondered. It wouldn't be good—he could bet on that.

"I met up with Ethan in town again yesterday. He was asking after those girls again. Wondering when they'd be coming back."

"What?" Luke stepped forward. "I don't want Mia to leave."

"He's not concerned with Mia," Ned said, meeting his father's gaze and holding it. "He just wants Fila off the ranch. Right, old man?"

"Don't old man me. But that's right. She's got no place here."

"I told you she has a place with me."

"And I'm telling you she doesn't." Holt pointed a finger at him. "She's not the one for you. Pack her things, send her home. I got a job for you that's going to take you out of town for a few days anyhow."

"I'm not sending her home." Ned raised his voice.

"Let me make this perfectly clear. She no longer lives

on the Double-Bar-K. Don't push me any further, Ned."

All went silent in the barn as the two of them faced off.

"I don't get it. You strong-armed Jake and Rob to get married. Now that I've found someone you're trying to break us up? Come on, Pop—where's my four week deadline? How come you're not offering me a chunk of the ranch to try to get me to marry her?"

"You want a deadline? I'll give you one. You've got one hour to get that foreigner off this ranch. And after you drop her off, you keep on driving. All the way to our hunting cabin."

"Why the hell would I go there?" The change of topic threw Ned off guard.

"Because the roof's about to collapse. Heard from Fitzgerald late last night. They've been getting snow and freezing rain alternating for the past week. It's piled up more than three feet, he says, solid ice between the layers of snow. His kid just came and picked him up to take him to his house for the rest of the winter."

"Damn," Jake muttered as they all exchanged glances. Fitzgerald was their closest neighbor at the hunting shack. Situated on a large acreage down a long dirt road in a remote area in the northwest corner of the state, the hunting cabin had been in the family for several generations. Most of the cabins up there were primitive affairs used intermittently during hunting season. Fitzgerald had turned his into a year-round abode after his wife died ten years ago. Most winters, his grown son ended up bailing him out when the snow got too deep, but he stayed as long as he could. He used his satellite phone to relay any emergencies to the Mathesons. If Fitzgerald said the roof was in danger of collapsing, he was serious.

"I want you to get up there and shovel off that roof before we lose the whole thing. Figure you'll be gone three to four days."

"That's not long enough to change my mind." Ned settled his hat more firmly on his head.

"Well, then maybe it'll be long enough to change hers. If you don't bring her back to Ethan's place, I will as soon as you're gone." No one spoke as Holt turned on his heel, walked out the barn door and slammed it behind him. All three of Ned's brothers watched him warily as if he might explode at any moment. Finally, Luke ventured, "I can't believe you didn't haul off and punch him for that. Or at least try to."

"You've changed," Jake said, consideringly. "I've had that thought before in the last few months, but this clinches it. When did you get a handle on your temper?"

"That doesn't matter. He ain't going to throw me off this ranch, no matter what he says." He looked from one to the other of his brothers. "You know he ain't."

"I don't know," Rob said. "I'm not sure he'll budge this time."

"I'm not taking Fila back to Ethan's. No way."

"I don't think I'd leave her here at Dad's mercy," Jake cautioned him. "Not for four days."

"Take her with you." When the others all turned to him, Luke shrugged. "It's the obvious solution."

"But you came up with it and you want me off this ranch, too," Ned said. "So what's up?"

Luke looked angry. "You're already going to be gone for four days. Who do you think is going to take up the slack while you're away? Me, that's who. I'm getting my chance. I plan to show Dad I'm way better at running things than you are. I don't have anything against you hooking up with Fila."

"So in other words, you'll screw Ned over until the cows come home when it comes to the ranch, but you're the first in line to support his love life?" Jake looked at him askance. "Or do you want Ned to stay with Fila so Dad will kick him out and you'll get it all?"

"I don't need to listen to this." Luke left as well.

"What do you think I should do?" Ned asked Jake.

"Actually, I think Luke's right; take her with you. If you leave her in Chance Creek, Dad will do something to screw with her while you're gone. I wouldn't put it past him to buy her a plane ticket, zip her into a suitcase and send her to Timbuktu."

Ned sighed. It was the truth. "She's supposed to be working on her restaurant."

"The tasting party is week from Saturday, right? You'll be back in plenty of time to set that up. Tell Fila to e-mail Hannah a plan for what needs to be done—shopping, prepping the restaurant, you name it. We'll split up the work and handle it while you're gone. She'll still have several days to finish up preparations when you get home. I'll tell Ethan and Autumn what happened today, too. I bet they have room for both of you at their place if Dad won't back down. Like you said, he wants us all to stay on the ranch. Maybe if you leave for a week or two, he'll think better of his methods. Things worked out for me and Rob. I bet they'll work out for you, too." Jake clapped him on the shoulder.

"How do I get him to change his mind about Fila?"

Neither brother could answer that.

"A SIX HOUR drive?" Fila repeated when Ned broke the news about going to the cabin. She hugged her arms across her chest trying to squelch the worry that had bloomed there since last night. Holt had made it all too clear he wanted her to leave. Going to a remote cabin would be a respite from him, but it wouldn't change anything permanently. She'd still have to deal with his dislike of her when they got back.

"Pack for more than four days, just in case," Ned told her. "Anything can happen up there. It might take a couple of days to get everything dug out and most of a day each way to travel. Bring shirts, pants, sweaters, underthings. Lots of warm gear."

Fila nodded reluctantly. She wondered if she should return to Ethan and Autumn's place instead. Surely going with Ned would just antagonize Holt more.

But she didn't want to give in to the old man, either. She wanted to stay with Ned. She'd grown accustomed to him.

"When you're done, would you check through what I've packed from the kitchen? You might think of something I've missed."

She nodded again. She headed upstairs, worry dogging her, but the act of packing calmed her somewhat. Maybe she and Ned could come up with a plan while they were there. Maybe the heavy physical work would distract her. Maybe fresh air and exercise were exactly what she needed, even if it meant going off into the wilderness.

She ended up repacking the kitchen gear entirely, taking out all the prepared boxed food Ned had included and substituting whole foods she could cook real meals from. That was one thing she hadn't gotten used to since coming home; the salt-laden fatty foods Americans seemed to subsist on. Even the ones she remembered fondly from her childhood tasted wrong now. She used to love macaroni and cheese. Now it tasted… well… awful.

"Ready? Let's get going," Ned said when he rejoined her.

Fila nodded, a thread of fear creeping in at the thought of the long drive, the unfamiliar terrain. The empty cabin. What if something happened to her? What if she was attacked? What if men with guns came and—

No. Autumn would call this catastrophic thinking, a phrase Fila understood even if she couldn't reliably spell it yet. Allowing a small fear to balloon into a huge one, until it blocked out common sense and made you act irrationally. There were no Taliban fighters here. She was in no danger with Ned.

Just like the famous quote Autumn had told her to remember, the only thing she had to fear was fear itself.

LATE THAT AFTERNOON, Ned threw his truck into 4 x 4 mode and drove off the main road onto an unmarked, snow-covered track that led into a sparse pine forest. A glance at Fila told him she was still sitting stiffly in the passenger seat, one hand now clinging to the handle of the door. She hadn't spoken much during their drive, which wasn't anything new, but still worried him. He knew she hadn't ridden in a vehicle much at all when she was in Afghanistan. The sensation still seemed to bother her. She probably didn't relish traveling into a remote, mountainous area in the dead of winter, either, but what could he do? He couldn't leave her back in Chance Creek.

"It's going to get bumpy for a while," he warned her. "Hang on, okay?"

"Are you sure this is safe?" she asked as he gunned the motor and powered through the deep snow on the track.

"I've done this a hundred times. It's slow going but we'll get there just fine."

It took nearly another hour and a half to advance the eighteen miles on the snow-covered dirt road to reach the steeply plunging driveway that led off of it to the left down to the cabin. He started down it carefully, but the truck's tires slid as the driveway curved and Ned cursed, hitting the gas and turning the wheel sharply to avoid sliding off the track.

A quick intake of breath told him he'd scared Fila again. Ned gritted his teeth and kept going, inching forward. The snow was deeper than he'd imagined down here. They might have trouble getting back out. He'd seen a weather report, though; temperatures were due to rise in a few days. The snow would melt, which meant the way out would still be bumpy, but passable. If they had to stay an extra day or two, so much the better. He could use the alone time with Fila.

"There it is," he said, pointing to the roof of the log cabin that had just come into view. "My father used to take us boys up here every year to give my mother a week of peace. We loved—shit!"

The driveway curved back up here and he had just goosed the engine again to plow through a particularly deep bank of snow when the truck hit a patch of hidden ice, stalled in place, then found purchase again and shot forward unexpectedly.

"Fila!" Ned shouted as they surged over the side of the

track. The land dropped sharply away and Ned braced himself as the truck fell through the air, then hit the earth nose-first with a crash that shook every bone in his body. The left front fender crumpled as it took the brunt of the impact and a searing pain ripped through Ned's leg. Something snapped. Fila shrieked as the truck flipped over, throwing Ned against its roof.

The world went black.

Chapter Fifteen

ROUGH HANDS SMOTHERED her in a burka, pulling the sky-blue fabric over her head and wrapping its folds around her so tightly she couldn't breathe.

Fila fought back, thrashing her arms and kicking her legs, but she was pinned in place, the fabric of the burka cutting off her air.

"Stop it!" she cried in Pashto, her mouth filling with soft, fuzzy fluff that choked her until she pushed it back with her tongue. "Stop!" Her mouth filled again and Fila writhed and fought, but the unseen captors' hands held her in place and her head pounded with her racing blood.

Once again she used her tongue to clear her mouth and this time she opened her eyes. When strength failed, it was time for cunning. Maybe if she relaxed, she'd fool her captors into letting go. She forced her muscles to go slack. At first the world was dark, as of course it would be beneath the all-covering burka. Where was the mesh that let her see out? Was the garment on backwards? Were they trying to kill her? She pushed back at the panic overwhelming her. One of her arms was pinned to her side, but the other was free. She began to feel around.

There was light but it was above her head, as if she was seeing out of a tunnel, and now that she thought about it, it wasn't burka cloth that surrounded her. This was too warm, too soft. It was…she batted with her free hand.

Her winter jacket, Fila realized with a start. She wasn't in Afghanistan, she was in Montana. In a truck, with Ned. She was…

Upside down.

The memory of their crash swept over Fila and she squirmed again, trying to put together the sequence of events. They'd slid over the side of the track, landed hard on the nose of the truck then tipped over altogether. She was hanging upside down, still strapped into her seatbelt, her thick winter jacket slipping up over her chin, her right arm pinned inside the straps of the seatbelt.

She had to calm down. Thrashing would only make it worse. She wiggled the fingers of both hands, then fumbled with her left hand to reach up and undo the jacket's zipper, high up over her face. She finally succeeded in unzipping it enough to allow cold fresh air to reach her nose and mouth. That was better. She could see a little, too.

Although that wasn't an improvement. The ceiling of the truck had buckled and now lay just inches from her face. To her right, the passenger side window had shattered. The shape of the frame was all wrong and she knew there was no way the door would open.

"Ned?" she croaked. She cleared her throat and tried again. "Ned? Are you there?" Her jacket blocked her view when she turned toward the driver's seat. She moved her head around, pushing the hood aside with her jaw and free hand as best she could. Finally, she spotted a crumpled shape that lay sprawled against the other side of the cab in a position that didn't seem possible for a human body to take. "Ned? Ned!"

He didn't move. She looked once more at his broken body and understood.

The accident had killed him.

She was alone.

A cold, hard lump of tears filled her throat but Fila swallowed them back. She knew how to conquer tears in a time of crisis. They got you nowhere in the little village where she'd spent her captivity. They didn't feed you or protect you from the cruel sidelong looks of the other women. They didn't clothe you when the wind howled around your shack or protect the skin of your fingers when you broke the ice in your washbowl at the beginning of another day.

First she must get free. Then she could face this new disaster that fate had thrown at her.

She realized that she was muttering one of the ancient protection prayers the village women often repeated. Well, why not? She needed as much protection now as they ever did. Her free hand searched for the seatbelt buckle and released it.

Remembering too late that it was all that held her aloft.

She hit the top of the cab with a hard thump that stung her scalp and shoulder. Claustrophobia gripped her as she realized how badly the cab had been crushed by the fall of the truck. Her only recourse was to slide out through the window where the glass had shattered. Muttering thanks for the thick protective cover of her winter coat, she did so slowly, wriggling and twisting until her body was free and she could extricate her legs.

Fila flopped back in the snow to catch her breath and

felt the first kiss of snowflakes touch her cheeks and nose. Staring up at a leaden sky between Lodgepole pines, she realized the snow and the cold were now her enemies again.

Ned.

Sitting up quickly, she moaned as the world tipped and tilted and the blood rushed in her ears. She braced herself against the cold ground until she'd regained her equilibrium and then crawled on all fours to the other side of the truck. The driver's side window was shattered as well, and she carefully cleaned away the shards until she could see inside. She hesitated before touching Ned. Knowing he was dead and seeing the truth of it were two entirely different things. She'd come to care for him deeply. She thought she might love him. She'd counted on there being enough time to learn more about him—and to master her fear of relationships. If she was honest she'd hoped someday they would be together.

She should have known better than to depend on there being that kind of time. Life changed in an instant—when you least expected it. Blink and the ones you loved were gone. Blink again and your own life hung by a thread. Fila blinked the sting of tears from her eyes, not that they'd fall. Not now when she needed to see clearly. She owed it to Ned to sit vigil by his death. To be a witness to it, so she could relay the circumstances to his family when she made it back to the ranch.

If she made it to the ranch.

She pushed that traitorous thought away. This was Montana, not Afghanistan. Ned had a cell phone. She'd make a phone call and someone would come and get them.

She touched Ned's face, turned toward her where he lay on the ceiling of the truck cab, one leg curled under him, the other heading in an unnatural direction. His face was still warm, of course, but not as warm as she would have liked.

She put her hand to his cheek. Comforting the dead.

Saying good-bye.

The stubble of his beard scraped her bare fingers and she drew a breath. She should have touched him more when he was alive. There'd been nothing to fear from this man; she saw that now.

Something feathered against her wrist and Fila froze. Air from the window? A breath of wind? She dipped her fingers to his neck to test his pulse. Nothing.

No—

Wait.

She pressed harder. Felt the thready rhythm of his blood pulsing through his veins.

Not dead!

Fila drove her head and shoulders through the window frame to get a better look. She held her hand under his nose. Yes, that was another breath.

Gulping back an aching sob, she plunged her hands under Ned's body as best she could, gripped his jacket and pulled.

It took long minutes to get him out of the truck. At one point he nearly woke. He tossed and turned his head, muttering unintelligibly. Fila tugged again, his broken leg jounced, Ned yelled and went unconscious.

Once he was free of the truck, she fished out the keys, slipped her own long jacket off, pushed and rolled and pulled at Ned until she'd laid him atop of it and used the sleeves to pull this makeshift sled along the ground. He slipped off of it again and again, until she had the idea of looping the coat-sleeves under his armpits. Still, she estimated it took nearly a half-hour to get him to the front door of the cabin. She thought she'd never get the large man up the three front steps and over the threshold and by the time his head hit the plank floor inside she was too far gone to worry about being gentle.

She manhandled him into the living room as close to the woodstove as possible then searched until she found newspaper, kindling and matches. She'd learned to start fires under worse conditions, so she was able to start one here without too much trouble. She fiddled with the flue until the fire drew well, and sat next to Ned to catch her breath.

In all her haste to get him inside and warm, she'd forgotten about his cell phone. She patted his clothing until she discovered it in his pocket. The glass screen was cracked, but the phone itself worked. Still, when she dialed the number for the Double-Bar-K, and then the Cruz ranch and then 9-1-1, she got no answer. They must be too far down this country road, she thought. Who knew the nearest place where she could get reception?

She tried going outside and even hiking up to the lane they'd drove in on, but it was no use. The cell phone didn't pick up any signal. She'd have to find another way to get help. But first she'd have to set Ned's leg or he could be crippled permanently.

The idea almost made her pass out. Like every other woman in her Afghan village, she'd learned the basics of first aid, and she'd often been made to assist an older woman who served as midwife and healer, as well. She'd witnessed bones being set many times over the years and as she grew older, she'd helped set them herself once or twice.

She'd never been the one in charge, however. The healer had told her where to sit, where to hold on and what to do. Now she was alone. She had no idea if she could do it right, but she knew she had to try. She found a small hatchet near the woodstove, went back outdoors and hunted around until she found two straight branches she could use for splints. She made quick work with the sharp tool to chop off small branches and bumps. Back indoors she found a well-worn sheet in the hall closet she could tear into strips.

Now came the tricky part. She surveyed Ned stretched out on the hard floor. He wore jeans, which she'd have to remove before she could set his leg and splint it. She'd never undressed a man before, though, and the thought left her sick with fear. What would Ned think of her when he knew? How could she touch a man in such a way? She hesitated for a long moment, wishing there was another choice, but she knew there wasn't. Autumn or Hannah wouldn't have wasted a second doing what needed to be done. What was modesty in the face of such an injury?

But Fila had been taught to value modesty above all else. She'd covered her face every time she left her compound's walls. She'd been afraid to even look at a man. Now she approached Ned's prone form and held her breath as she undid his belt buckle and the button of his pants. She almost closed her eyes when she unzipped them. Beneath his jeans he wore dark blue boxer briefs that didn't cover nearly enough of his anatomy, to her point of view. She remembered the village healer and her brusque mannerism when she treated her patients. Fila fought for a similar composure, but touching Ned like this brought a rush of sensations to her body she hardly understood. Even in unconsciousness, Ned was all male. He posed no threat to her in this condition, which allowed her, in turn, to take a breath and appreciate him in a way she never had before. He was well-formed. Broad in the chest and shoulders. Strong of jaw. As she slid and tugged the jeans off of him as gently as she could, she revealed powerful thighs. They were thick with muscle, covered with a thatch of wiry hair. His briefs bulged in interesting places, but she tore her gaze away from them and focused on the job at hand.

There was no time to explore Ned's body. To do so without his approval would be wrong, anyway. Still as she turned away, she longed to look again. She found him utterly fascinating, and with no danger of him responding to her glances, it seemed a shame to waste such an opportunity.

She only allowed herself one more quick look, however, before she moved her attention to his legs. It was obvious where the break occurred—in his left thigh. It was a bad one, too.

Ned needed her to be practical now. To be professional, as much as she could be. She needed to brace his body somehow and tug his leg sharply to snap the broken bone back into place. Toward the back of the large living room, a thick, wooden post braced up a ceiling beam. Fila decided she could make use of it. She searched the cabin until she found a long length of inch-thick rope. She edged Ned as close to the post as she could, then hauled and tugged him into a seated position, wrapping the rope around and around his torso as tightly as she could to bind him to the post. The result reminded her of cartoons she'd seen as a child, in which villains tied up unsuspecting maidens in coils of ropes that only left their head and feet sticking out, and left them lying on railway tracks. The loops of rope covered Ned from his hips to his armpits. She wasn't sure this would work, but didn't know what else to do.

Kneeling down at his feet, Fila tentatively took his left foot in her hand, sucked in a breath, screwed up her courage and jerked back as hard as she could. She felt the bones of his thigh snap into position and she released his foot with an exhale, nearly overwhelmed with nausea. Had she done it right? She didn't think she had the courage to try it again. She inched closer to Ned, thankful he was still out cold. She felt along his thigh carefully, pressing his skin harder as she gained in confidence. All felt in place, so she quickly positioned the splints and bound his leg firmly. When she was done, she sat back, breathing deeply. Her brow was damp with sweat and her hands trembled. Suddenly, the enormity of her position crashed over her. She was alone with an injured man, far from civilization. Her phone didn't work and she didn't know if Ned's injury might become infected or worse. Fear clogged her throat and her breathing sped up until she was almost hyperventilating. She bent forward until her forehead touched the floor, tears finally spilling over her eyes.

After a long minute, she forced herself to straighten up. Scraping her sleeve over her eyes she vowed to herself it was the last time she'd cry until she was home at the Double-Bar-K again. She had to stay strong. For herself—and for Ned.

NED WOKE TO an ache in his thigh so intense he thought he'd throw up. His head pounded, his tongue was thick and he was lying on a cold hard floor that did little to improve things. He twisted his head to try to make out his location and was rewarded with a throb of pain through his temples that nearly took his breath away.

He lay still until the room stopped spinning and tried again. Above him were the bare wooden rafters of a ceiling of a rustic cabin. Below him his fingers traced over rough-hewn plank boards. There was something familiar about the fireplace and the taxidermied buck's head that hung above the mantel.

This was his family's place—their hunting cabin.

Suddenly it all came back in a rush.

Fila. Where was Fila?

He tried to sit up but the pain forced him down again before he'd barely moved an inch. His thigh was on fire and his forehead damp with sweat. His whole body felt like he'd been tossed from a bucking bronco. He was in bad shape—literally flat on his back—but he hadn't moved himself here. He hoped that meant Fila wasn't nearly hurt as bad.

Memories assailed him, driving a groan from his throat. He'd driven right off the road.

He could have killed them both.

Like an idiot he hadn't buckled himself in during their ride from Chance Creek. Seatbelt laws irritated him, as did anything that attempted to restrict his liberties. Now he wished he'd restricted his own damn liberties a little bit.

What if he'd hurt Fila? What if she was dead, even? Someone else could have found them and dragged him in here.

He tried again to sit up and this time made it halfway before white fuzz spiked through his vision and a resounding thump through his skull a moment later told him he'd passed out and crashed back again.

He felt footsteps through the floor boards, light but firm. Someone was approaching. He opened one eye and a wave of relief crashed over him. "Fila," he said.

"Yes," she said. "I'm well. You are hurt." Her soft voice chided him. Well, he deserved it, didn't he?

"Did you call for help?"

"There's no signal, not even outside."

Ned closed his eyes. Of course—not out here. They were never able to get a signal until they'd traveled out to the highway and some miles south. The hunting lodge was designed to be remote. Part of its charm was its lack of access to the outside world.

"The truck?"

She shook her head. He believed her. It had to be totaled after the fall from the driveway. "I'm sorry," he made himself say. He didn't often apologize, but this time it seemed warranted. He wanted to say more, but the words didn't come. Flat here on his back, it was all too apparent how big an idiot he'd allowed himself to become. He'd wanted to rescue Fila—protect her from her fears, build her a whole new life—and now look what he'd done.

"I'm fine. You broke your leg. I don't know if you are hurt in other places."

Ned wasn't sure either. His hands and arms seemed to be intact. He touched his chest and stomach and hips. All was right with them, too. Some sore spots which were probably bruises, but that was it. When his hands reached beneath the covers she'd piled on top of him, however, he realized what was different.

His pants. He no longer wore jeans. These were…a loose pair of sweat pants. He reached down farther, found where she'd split them up the leg. Took in the hard sticks that acted as splints beneath them. He cocked an eyebrow at her.

Fila blushed.

His own body fired up in response. Fila had undressed him? Had she liked what she saw?

"I set the bone," Fila said, quenching his interesting thoughts, "but it could get infected."

"You set it?" He wished he could sit up and look her head on. Wanted to ask her about his pants, but on the other hand, didn't. If his leg was broken, the break had to be where it now throbbed and buzzed halfway down his thigh. His leg felt stiff too, and he realized that she'd splinted it in lieu of a cast. How on earth could a slip of a girl like Fila set his thigh? Maybe it hadn't been broken that badly.

When he said as much to her, however, she shook her head gravely. "It was like this when I found you," she said, demonstrating with two fingers. One pointed down like a leg should. The other one bent to the side. Ned's stomach lurched.

"How did you know what to do?"

"I helped several times in my village. In Afghanistan," she explained. "There was no doctor there. The older women knew what to do. We younger ones helped them. We held them down."

"The patients?"

She nodded. "You were unconscious. Much easier. I tied you to the post."

The post, huh? Ned was getting an entirely new admiration for her. Setting a leg took strength. "Glad you did it while I was out cold." He wondered if she had done it right, though. It sure hurt like hell. And what had she said about infection? What would they do if that happened?

"I must go get help," she said as if reading his mind.

"You can't."

"The snow isn't so deep," she assured him. "I'll build up the fire and leave you food and something to drink. Blankets."

"You can't," he reiterated. "There's no one else out here. It's eighteen miles to the road and that's the closest we ever get reception. You'd have to camp overnight somewhere on the way—in sub-freezing weather. Then, when you reached the highway, who knows who'd stop for you? What if it's the wrong kind of person? Uh uh. You have to stay here. My family will come after us."

"When?" she demanded.

"I said we'd be gone for four days."

"So we wait all that time?"

Ned shrugged and looked away. "I guess. What's wrong—afraid to be alone with me?" He regretted the taunt as soon as he said it. This wasn't some girl he was hitting on at the Dancing Boot. This was Fila. She'd been through far too much to tease.

"I'm afraid you'll die if that break gets infected." She was angry.

"Let's just hope it doesn't get infected then." He turned his head. The floor was uncomfortable. "Any chance I could get a pillow?"

Fila disappeared and came back with one. She brought another comforter, too, and laid it over him. The slightest movement or pressure on his leg was agony and he knew he was in for a very long haul until someone came after them. Fila was right, too; it could be days. His family knew he was usually capable of looking after himself. They knew, too, that he preferred to spend time alone every now and then. His best bet was that someone would worry about Fila out in the wilderness with him and come to fetch her early. Maybe they'd worry enough to come today.

Fila built up the fire and soon he was warm except for his back on the cool floorboards. When he mentioned it, Fila started the slow process of lifting him an inch at a time and insinuating another comforter between him and the planks. Each jostle to his leg made him wince and sweat. When she was finally done his nausea had returned.

She disappeared again and came back with a bottle of pain reliever. After consulting together, she gave him several tablets and lifted his head and shoulders so he could sip some water without drowning himself.

"Rest now," she told him, as if he had any choice. He caught her hand as she got up to put the medicine away.

"Thank you," he said. "It couldn't have been easy to get me inside. You're very brave."

"Not as brave as you think." She tugged her hand free.

Chapter Sixteen

NOW THAT NED was settled and out of danger for the moment, Fila dressed back up in her warm coat and boots and went outside to bring in their provisions. She found their duffel bags thrown clear of the truck and hauled them indoors one at a time. Their groceries and ice chest hadn't fared so well. The milk and most of the cooking oil had drained out of their containers. The eggs were crushed. But the dry goods and butter were fine. She collected the containers and bags where they were strewn around the upside-down truck, then peered inside its cab again to see what she might have missed.

She spotted an ancient-looking first aid kit near the back of the cab and figured it used to be stowed under the driver's seat. Fishing it out, she opened it and found several things that might come in handy. She packed it in with the groceries and brought everything inside.

Ned had stuffed the pillow under his head and neck to raise himself up a little and he watched her move around the cabin unpacking the bags and setting things to rights. She set a pot of water to boil to make him tea on the old-fashioned iron cookstove and wished she had some herbs on hand with antibiotic properties. Or antibiotics themselves.

That reminded her of the first aid kit. She brought it out and went through it but although it contained antiseptic wipes and rubber gloves, it contained nothing he could take for an interior infection. Fila's worry grew.

There was nothing for it; she'd have to hike out first thing in the morning. She'd leave before first light and go fast to make it to the highway before the sun set again. She'd bring the cell phone and call for a rescue the minute she got service. Or she'd flag down a passing vehicle and find help that way.

The whole idea left her numb with dread. She didn't fear the forest road, exactly—it was too cold for bears and she thought most other animals would leave her alone. Unless there were wolves; she feared wolves. She feared strangers, too. She'd need to flag some down on the highway, however, if it turned out she still couldn't get reception. Ned was right; she had no idea who would stop for her.

And if she had to spend the night outside? How would she manage that? She could freeze to death before she ever got help for Ned.

"Did you check the roof?" Ned said, interrupting her thoughts.

"The roof of the truck?" She hated to think how close both of them had come to being crushed.

"The roof of the house. Remember why we came here in the first place?"

She hadn't remembered. Not after the horrific accident and the even worse experience of setting Ned's leg. She tried to picture the exterior of the cabin in her mind. She had an impression of a snow covered roof, but had no idea how deep that snow was.

"You'd better go outside and take a look," Ned said.

She wrapped up once again and did so. She trudged out into the yard, turned around and nearly stifled a groan. At least two feet of snow had accumulated on top of the little building—maybe closer to three. She returned inside and reported her findings to Ned. He looked grave.

"If there is ice layered in between the snow up there it will be heavy as heck," he said. "We've got shovels and picks in the shed out back. You'll have to do what you can." He must have seen the look on her face. "Sorry, Fila. I hate to ask you to do all the work, but I don't think I'll be much help."

"No." She shook her head, knowing she had to do whatever it took to keep Ned lying down and resting. "How do I get up there?"

NED GROANED AS he listened to Fila's tentative shoveling on the roof above his head. He couldn't stand the thought of her up there doing such heavy work alone. He was the one that should be shoveling, while she remained safe and warm inside. Of all the stupid things he'd ever done, flipping his truck took the cake. He'd never live it down. If he got out of here. It worried him that his leg could get infected—but not for his own sake. If it withered and fell off it would be his own damn fault. But if things got bad enough, Fila might try to make that hike out to the main road and that was dangerous—too dangerous.

Her shovel chipped away at the snow above him, the repetitive clunks telling him his neighbor had been right;

there were layers of ice between the snow. It would be hard to break through and get off of the roof, but if left there, the whole thing could collapse. With him underneath it.

The pain reliever he'd taken had barely dulled the ache in his leg, and as the minutes crept by, Ned's spirits sunk. He had no television to lighten things up. There were books, but even if he could fetch them he'd barely be able to make head or tails of their contents. The forced stillness gave him much too much time to think about his life. He really had messed up this time. Forget about managing the cattle herd now—Luke was about to get his chance, after all. As usual, Ned would be screwed.

He heard the bang and rattle of the metal ladder against the house. Fila must be coming down. He waited and sure enough, she came through the front door several minutes later.

"How's it going?" He watched her kick off her boots and strip off her jacket. She pinned her gloves to a clothes rack near the front door to dry and entered the living room.

"Slow." She sighed. "I'm not strong enough." She rubbed her wrists as she sat down on the sofa.

"You're plenty strong. I've seen the muscles in your arms when you knead dough."

She made a face. "Shoveling ice and snow is harder than making bread. Still, I'll do it—I just can't do it all at once. I need a break." She sat back against the pillows.

"Relax for a while, then. Take a nap."

She shook her head, got up and crossed the room to the bookcase. After perusing the shelves for a moment, she pulled out a slim volume. Ned frowned. Was she going to ignore him while she read? A spurt of anger pulsed through him at the thought she'd rather read than talk to him, but he stifled it. It wasn't Fila's fault he was flat on his back. He wanted to ask her what book she'd chosen, but usually when he asked that, people didn't answer him. Instead they held the book up so he could read the title.

Which told him nothing.

"It's an adventure story." Fila crossed back to the couch and sat down. She tucked her feet up under her and positioned the pillows behind her back. "The Call of the Wild, by Jack London."

"I think I've seen the movie."

"Should I read it out loud to pass the time?" When he didn't answer right away, she sighed. "I know it's for younger readers, but I'm not very good."

"Not very good at what?" Ned shifted to see her better and gritted his teeth against the pain.

"At reading. I haven't been in school in over ten years, so there are lots of words in adult books that are unfamiliar. I can usually figure them out, but I'm kind of slow."

That made sense. Funny he hadn't thought of it before. "Did you learn to read Arabic?"

"Actually, the Afghans speak Pashto, among many other tribal languages. Not Arabic. But no, I didn't read at all once I got there. There was nothing to read in my village. Plus it wouldn't be allowed."

"Huh." Maybe he'd found the one woman who couldn't lord her superior learning over him. "Yeah, sure. Go ahead and read some." It would pass the time.

"Just a few pages," she said. "Then I'll go back outside."

They nearly didn't make it through the first page. Fila handled the chapter heading easily enough, but then came the verse of a poem—an old one, judging by the language.

She sounded it out as best she could, but it left both of them puzzled with its archaic terms.

"Maybe I'll pick another book," Fila said.

"It was a good movie," Ned said. "About a dog. I like dogs. Try the first few lines. Maybe it gets better."

It did. They were introduced to Buck, a happy, yellow dog who lived in 1897 that made Ned think of Boomer. A page later, they read of the hired hand who stole him from his master and used him to pay off a gambling debt. By the third page Buck was riding a train bound for San Francisco with a rope around his neck. Fila looked sympathetic. Ned reckoned she could relate to the way a life could be so quickly overturned. Right now he could, too.

She read two more pages, struggling with some of the words, having an easy time with others. She put the book down with a sigh. "I'll try again." She pointed to the roof.

"Thanks for reading. It did help pass the time. Buck sounds like my old dog—Boomer."

"What happened to him?"

"He got hit by a car." Ned remembered the way the dog used to nudge his hand with his nose when he wanted to be petted—reminding Ned he was there, ready for anything.

Ned let his head fall back to the floor. He'd break those truck windows all over again if it meant he could have Boomer back. Then he thought about Cab's ultimatum. No, he wouldn't—but he missed Boomer.

"After dinner we can read more."

"Uh huh," Ned said distractedly. A glance out the window told him the afternoon was waning. "You come down before it gets dark."

"I will."

Soon he was alone again, but at least he had something to think about. A yellow dog kidnapped from its home. He had a vague memory of the plot of the movie, but had lost many of the details. He liked the way the story was told from the dog's point of view. That was clever. Boomer had been clever, too.

He wished his dog was here now. He could sure use the company.

As the chip, chip, chip of Fila's shovel started up over his head, Ned's eyes drifted closed. His leg hurt, the floor beneath him was hard, but all wasn't lost. He was alone with Fila and they'd shared something together—the story read-aloud. When he thought about it, she seemed calmer, too, than she'd been in the past few weeks. She was too busy taking care of him to remember her own fears. Ned considered this. Maybe breaking his leg would have an upside. Maybe she'd get over the past while she cared for him. He'd lie on this floor forever if it meant she'd heal enough to fall in love with him.

FILA'S FINGERS WERE so sore she could barely grip the ladder when she climbed down again two hours later. She was discouraged as well as aching when she realized she'd barely shoveled a third of the snow off the back half of the roof. She'd have to start in again first thing in the morning and pray the structure held up through the night.

When she made it back inside, the cabin was dark except for a dim glow from the wood stove.

"I'm sorry." She hurried into the living room once her outer gear was off. "I should have thought to light a lamp."

"There's an oil lamp on that table." Ned pointed toward the back of the room. "Should be matches close by."

She found them, trimmed the wick and got the lamp burning. As its light filled the room, she relaxed a little. That was better. She brought a glass of water to Ned, but he waved it away. "What I need is crutches. I think there might be an old pair up in the attic."

"Crutches? You can't walk." Fila was adamant.

"I can, too. I need to go to the head." Another thing she hadn't thought of. "Take the lamp with you. I'll be okay." He pointed to the stairs and she made her way up them, shining the lamp ahead of her. The loft was a small, cramped, cobwebby space packed with odds and ends. After shifting piles of old gear she finally unearthed a primitive pair of wooden crutches and brought them back downstairs.

Ned struggled to stand and it took all her strength to brace him while he did. By the time he was on his feet, his face was white and he was sweating. Once the crutches were braced under his arms, however, he did better. He swung himself around and down the short hall to the bathroom.

Several minutes later, he was back. Instead of taking up a position on the floor, however, he hovered in the hall. "You think it's a bad idea if I try the bed?"

Fila thought hard. "It's important to keep your leg straight."

"I think if you position some pillows around it, I can do that."

She assented silently, and when he was settled on the double bed in the main bedroom she agreed it was better than having him lie on the floor.

"Much better," he said. "Keep those crutches where I

can reach them."

"Only to go to the bathroom. Otherwise you sit still."

"Believe me," Ned said. "I have no plans to go for a stroll."

She could believe it. He looked strained. Obviously in pain. She fetched the pain reliever tablets she'd found earlier and gave him more. She wished she had something stronger.

"I'll make dinner."

"Looking forward to it."

Soon they were holding warm bowls of homemade *dal* and dunking biscuits in the thick lentil soup. Ned still sat on the bed with his legs stretched out before him, Fila perched on a folding chair she'd brought in from the main room. It was a plain meal, but a filling one. In some ways, sitting in the glow of the oil light in an otherwise dark, and not altogether warm house reminded her of her time in Afghanistan. The old wood-fired cookstove in the kitchen sure did.

"Thinking of your time away?"

Fila nodded.

Ned shifted a little. Winced. "Did they hurt you, Fila?"

It was the question everyone wanted answered. Did they hurt her? She hesitated before saying, "I was not raped."

Ned didn't look away. "I'm glad to hear that. That doesn't entirely answer the question, though."

Tears pricked her eyes. She blinked them back, remembering her vow. "I don't think I can put into words what they did."

"Try."

She set the bowl down on the bedside table and clasped

her hands together in her lap. "They took away...everything. My family. My home. My country. They kept...saying I was wrong. Everything I did was wrong. Everything I felt was wrong. Everything I thought was wrong. Until I didn't know what was wrong or right anymore." She took a deep, shuddering breath. "It was like being peeled away layer by layer by layer until there was nothing left. Until I became nothing. Until I disappeared. I thought when I came home I'd get it all back again, but—" She shook her head. "There's nothing to get back. Who I was—" A tear trailed its way down her cheek, despite her best efforts. "It's gone." Her voice cracked and she fought for composure, her fingers entwined so tightly together they ached.

Ned didn't need to know all this. She didn't want him to know it. The words still spilled from her lips, though. "Now it's just the same here as it was there. Everything I do is wrong. Everything I say and think and the ways I react. The way I look—it's all wrong. I don't fit in here any more than I fit there. They won!" Her voice spiked upward as she put voice to her worst fear.

Ned tried to reach for her, swore when the motion jostled his leg, put down his bowl and finally touched her hand. "They did not win." His voice was nearly a growl. "You got away from them. You didn't become one of them. If they'd won you'd have a suicide vest strapped on and be marching into some crowded building. All that's happening right now is you're readjusting to coming home. Soldiers go through the same damn thing, you know. That's what you're like—a soldier coming home. A prisoner of war." Fila scraped the wetness from her cheeks with her sleeve. She hadn't looked at it that way. He touched her again. "You've been to war for over a decade. Give yourself time." He patted her knee. "And for God's sake, go ahead and scream once in a while. Cry. Throw things. Let it out."

"I can't."

"You're going to have to."

He didn't understand. No one did. Sometimes she thought she would start screaming and never be able to stop again. When she thought about what happened, how much she'd lost—how much time she'd lost—it made her feel like shredding the things that surrounded her into a thousand pieces. She didn't know what to do with her anger. It was almost worse than her fear.

"Go on and eat. You probably worked up an appetite shoveling off that roof," Ned said. "Think I could get another bowl of that soup? It's good."

"Of course." She gathered their dishes and stood.

"By the way," Ned said casually. "The way you look is not all wrong. You're the most beautiful woman I've ever seen."

Fila quickly darted to the kitchen and spent far more time than necessary spooning more soup for each of them from the pot on the small cook stove. The knowledge that Ned thought she was pretty—beautiful, actually—warmed her all the way through.

Chapter Seventeen

NED SAT BACK against the pillows Fila had placed between his back and the headboard of the bed, his leg aching. Fila perched cross-legged on the kitchen chair she'd dragged into the room at dinnertime and read more from *The Call of the Wild*. While he enjoyed the story—he liked dogs, history and action—he couldn't rid himself of the nagging worry that sooner or later she'd address his inability to read as well as he should.

It galled him that a man could ride a horse, help oversee a ranch, build and repair all kinds of equipment, predict the weather from natural signs, and do most any chore on a large cattle spread and all anyone judged him by was his inability to decipher the printed word. He'd worked hard to make up for that one little deficiency and still it seemed to define him. No wonder he was quick-tempered.

Fila had a beautiful voice and he could tell she liked the story, too. She sped up in the action parts and grew angry whenever Buck the dog was hard done by. Which was often. He had a feeling she identified with that dog as much as he did. Finally, she cleared her throat. "I have to stop. I'm losing my voice."

Ned nodded, his body tensing. Here's where most people would ask him to take over and read aloud. He had a hunch that Fila had figured out his problem, but he wasn't sure. He figured he'd find out now.

"Time for bed," she said, surprising him. He checked his watch. Had it really gotten that late? "Do you want a snack first? Some more soup?"

"I'm fine. I could use more of that pain reliever, though."

She went and fetched the bottle of pills and a fresh glass of water, then watched him wash down two.

"I'll sleep in the other room."

Ned shook his head. "The bunk room? You'll freeze to death in there. No way. You'll sleep right here with me, so I know you're safe. We'll help keep each other warm."

She shook her head quickly. "I couldn't."

"Look, I'm no danger to you." He pointed to his leg.

She hesitated a long moment. "It wouldn't be right."

"You had your own room in Afghanistan?"

"No. But I never slept alone with a man, either."

"Fila, I get it—you're right, normally it wouldn't be a good idea. I might take advantage of the situation." He flashed her a wolfish grin. "But not tonight. Not like this."

She cocked her head. "You'd...take advantage?"

A smile twitched his lips. "You'd better believe it. I'd chase you all over this cabin if I had to."

She ducked her head, hiding her own smile. "I run very fast."

"Not as fast as me, I bet."

"I bet I am."

When she peeped up at him, her eyes were dancing with humor. Ned felt a rush of tenderness. "I'll race you any time. As soon as my leg heals up."

"All right," she said softly.

"All right?"

"I'll sleep here tonight."

He squashed the urge to whoop with the victory. He doubted he'd get any sleep himself between the pain in his leg and the knowledge she was so close, but it was worth it to have her near. He could listen to her breathing and smell the scent of her soap. He could dream, too, of a time when her fear was gone. When they could meet as man and woman without the past standing between them.

He struggled to the washroom again, then settled himself on the bed as comfortably as he could. Fila fluttered around him, doing all she could to help until he waved her away. "There should be a flashlight under your side of the bed. We try to keep them stocked."

"I found it," she said a moment later. She disappeared into the bathroom and came out some minutes later in a pair of yoga pants and a fleecy top. He was glad to see she had something warm to sleep in, although he'd vastly prefer it if nothing lay between them. He'd keep her real warm, then.

As Fila climbed carefully between the covers next to him on the opposite side from his hurt leg, the movement of the bed jostled him and set it to aching again. But when her shoulder rubbed up against his, the shock of the contact banished all thoughts of pain from his head. She quickly scooted away, making sure to leave several inches between them.

"It's all right to come closer," he said, although he knew she wouldn't. "I don't bite."

"You might." She peeped up at him from underneath

the covers when he turned his head. Only her eyes were visible, but he was pretty sure she was smiling under there.

He smiled back. "You're right; I might. If I could reach you. But I can't. And it's cold. Come over here."

To his surprise, she did as she was told. Inching closer to him, she turned on her side and curled against him. He could smell the citrus scent of her shampoo, and feel her fingers wrapped around his bicep. Her soft, warm presence against him was heavenly, and his body began to react to it in predictable ways.

Ned shifted uncomfortably.

Fila peeped up at him again. "Go to sleep."

Ned chuckled. That wasn't likely. Not with a beautiful young woman so close at hand, yet so unattainable. A long pause ensued, broken only by their breathing. Ned began to feel that this night might be more uncomfortable than he thought, when Fila finally broke the silence.

"What are your plans, Ned? Everyone always asks me about mine."

His plans? They'd changed since she'd entered his life. Before then he'd figured he'd make his way through the world alone, since his relationships with women had always been short and unsatisfactory. Now he knew he'd never be happy without Fila by his side. "My dreams are simple. I want to run my family's ranch. I want to find a wife. I want to raise a family, maybe."

"What kind of wife?" She buried her face against his arm.

"A beautiful one who'll cook *bolani* for me morning, noon and night."

She stilled. Moved away from him. "I can't be anyone's wife, Ned."

"Why not?" He wanted to scoot across the bed after her, but he couldn't—not with this damn leg.

"Because I'm not… whole. I'm no good."

Ned let out a huff of air. "Fila, I've been told I'm no good practically all my life. I've decided not to believe it anymore. Maybe you should try it."

She stiffened. "You're good!"

"You're about the only one who thinks so. Everyone else thinks I'm a mess."

"They don't know you."

"And you do?"

She nodded her head vigorously.

"Well, I think I know you as well as you do me, and I say you're good, too. You're a little mixed up, a little overwhelmed with coming home, but that's all. You'd do just fine if you relaxed a little."

"You mean if I opened a restaurant so I could earn lots of money."

Ned was taken aback by the censure in her voice. "I don't know about earning lots of money—the restaurant business is tricky—but enough so you have some choices. Fila, I think you should find out what you like to do best and pursue it. Maybe that's running a restaurant, maybe it isn't. You're scared now, but you won't always be. You're strong. Strong women don't stay down for long."

"What if I don't get better?"

"You have to. I need you." Time to lay it all out for her. "I'm not going to push you, but someday I'm going to ask you to marry me. You'd better be prepared to say yes."

She turned away from him, and he thought he'd angered her, but she scooted closer until her backside pressed against him. "I'm not ever getting married."

"We'll see about that."

Chapter Eighteen

THE NEXT MORNING passed as slow as molasses for Ned. He'd slept fitfully through the night, waking several times to listen to Fila's quiet breathing. He was touched that she trusted him enough to sleep so soundly. He wished that he could do the same. He was worried about the roof, though. Worried about Fila, too. What if she fell when she was shoveling? What if she hurt herself?

He'd never forgive himself then.

When Fila got up, she slid shyly out of bed, disappeared into the bathroom to change and brought a plate of breakfast to him some minutes later, but declined to sit and eat with him. Instead, she ate quickly in the kitchen and dressed in her warm outer gear in preparation to climb back on the roof. He listened to her chipping away at the ice up there for the rest of the morning, trying hard to be grateful that all was going so well, but as time passed at a glacial pace he found it hard not to slide into grim thoughts. What would happen when they returned to the ranch? Would Fila's newfound confidence stick? Would Holt throw them out?

He wasn't prepared to think about that last question.

Fila took one look at him when she came in at lunchtime and went right back out to the living room to gather two or three hunting magazines and place them in his lap.

"What am I supposed to do with these?" Ned's voice was gruffer than he meant it to be.

"Look at the pictures. It's better than nothing."

He set them aside. "Don't you need a break? You could read to me."

She nodded. "But I can't stay too long. I'm not even close to done with this half of the roof."

"Don't hurt yourself."

"I'm used to hard work." But she picked up the novel and Ned's mood improved. At least the story helped to pass the time. His leg's dull ache wasn't anything for him to gripe about—it was his own damn fault he'd broken it—but the silence and forced idleness were beginning to take its toll.

"Did you ever have a dog?" he thought to ask her.

"Of my own? No." The idea seemed to surprise her. "In the village they weren't pets. They were for protection. They were always hungry…" She trailed off and he got the picture.

"That's a shame." Stuck in the cabin alone, he missed Boomer more than he cared to admit. It was probably time to get a new pet. He'd have to check out the Chance Creek Animal Shelter when he was back on his feet.

He sat back and listened to Fila read for twenty minutes. All too soon, she shut the book and placed it on the bed.

"You're leaving?"

"I have to. That roof won't shovel itself."

He knew it was important that she relieve the weight up there, but he didn't relish being alone again.

"Fila?"

"What?"

"Kiss me."

Her eyebrows shot up and her face flushed. Ned grabbed her hand before she could dash from the room.

"Don't you want to kiss me?"

Her color heightened. She kept her gaze on the floor, her long, lush eyelashes fanning against her cheeks. After a moment she nodded her head.

"Come here, then."

She bent closer. Ned shifted to meet her and they kissed. Softly at first—he didn't want to scare her—but as the seconds passed, he turned up the heat. Sliding a hand up behind her head, he asked more of her, moving his mouth over hers, nipping at her lips, finally pressing for entry with his tongue.

She gasped and pulled back. He let her go. Waited.

A few moments later she was back for more.

It wasn't the most comfortable position and after a minute or two, Ned's leg began to ache again. He didn't care. He'd put up with almost anything if it meant this sweet torture would carry on. Finally, breathless, they pulled apart. Fila ducked her head, but he cupped her chin and lifted it until her gaze met his.

"I like you, Fila Sahar."

A smile broke over her face like a radiant dawn. "I like you, too."

He sealed the moment with a quick final kiss. "You'd better get back to it. Wish I could help."

She nodded and slipped from the room.

SHE'D KISSED NED. Really kissed him—not just an innocent kiss on the cheek. She'd kissed him like a woman in love kissed a man.

She wanted to do it again.

Fila cradled the new, exciting feeling to her chest as she wrapped up in layers and braved the cold again. Climbing up to the roof, she surveyed the area she'd already cleared, and the much greater expanse of roof still to go. She'd shoveled about two-thirds of the side of the roof that covered the bedrooms and kitchen, but there was still a third to do, and then all of the side that covered the open living room area. The thought of all the work ahead left her almost too tired to get started.

As she got to it, she replayed the kiss again and again, her whole body tingling in delightful ways. In frightening ways, too. She had to constantly remind herself that here in America it was fine for her to feel this way about Ned.

At least according to everyone except Holt. He wouldn't approve.

Was there anything she could do to change his mind? Dye her hair blond, maybe?

She smiled despite the seriousness of the question. That probably wouldn't work, but somehow she had to convert Holt to her side, because she didn't want to make Ned unhappy, which he would be if he was forced to choose between them.

And she didn't mean to give him up, either.

She turned the question around in her mind over and over again as she chipped away at the ice and snow. Should she concentrate on being more American? Dressing like the others? Mimicking the way they talked and moved? Learning everything she could about the ranch? Asking Lisa to teach her to cook all his favorite meals?

Would her restaurant be a constant source of irritation to Holt if she served Afghan food? Should she turn it into a steak house?

No—then she'd compete directly with DelMonaco's. Besides, she had no idea how to cook steaks. Afghan food was her specialty.

She shook her head. She'd just spent a decade conforming to a group of men's ideas about ideal womanhood. She hadn't escaped just to come here and do the same thing all over again. She'd do what she could to build peace between herself and Holt, but she wouldn't change for him.

He'd have to accept her the way she was.

NED LISTENED TO the sounds of Fila on the roof chipping away at the snow. Over the course of the last hour her movements had gotten slower, the quiet spaces when she rested in between getting longer. He was worried about her, and truth be told, he was worried about the cabin, too. That load of snow and ice had to be putting a lot of stress on the old trusses that held up the roof. He hoped like hell it didn't all come down on top of them.

When he wasn't worried about the roof, he replayed that kiss in his mind. It hadn't disappointed him. Far from it—he now burned with the desire to experience more with Fila. He had to be patient, though. No sense pushing things too far. He had to let her get used to him slowly. He could do that.

Even if it killed him.

When Fila finally came back in she took some time getting her outer gear off before making her way to the bunk room to check on him. Her hair was flecked with water and the collar of her shirt was wet.

"Is it raining?"

She nodded. "Freezing rain. It just started, but it got really slippery really fast."

Ned tamped down a spurt of worry. That was all they needed—more ice on top of the layers already up on that roof.

"I'm almost done with this side of the roof. Almost but not quite." She sat in the chair beside his bed. He could tell she was thoroughly worn out.

"I'm sure you're doing great." Ned glanced up at the ceiling. Above them lay the attic, the roof trusses and the roof itself. He was glad to know the snow was mostly off the side above them. The other side—over the living room and dining room—was still fully laden. It had to be an awfully heavy load.

"I'm working too slow."

"It'll get done. Don't worry." He was worried, though. She'd have to go back on the roof after lunch, even if it was still raining.

"I'll get some of that soup."

"Great," Ned said absently. He half-listened to her move about the kitchen, the distant clang of pots and dishes forming a backdrop for his thoughts. Was there a better way to get the snow off the roof? A better tool to use to break through the ice?

"Do you want tea?" Fila appeared around the door-frame. "I found some in the—"

With a roar like a tidal wave, the cabin shook, nearly pitching Ned from his bed. He held onto its frame for dear life as Fila lurched forward, fell to her knees and clung to the chair by his bedside.

"What is it?" she shouted.

"The roof." Ned reached for her. The part over the living room was caving in. Any minute the rest of it would come down. "Fila!"

She clawed closer, grabbing his hand as another crash shook the foundation. Ned leaned over the edge of the bed and wrapped his arms around her, trying to shield her from falling debris, clenching his jaw against the pain in his thigh at every movement and shudder from the house.

"Fila!"

She reared up and caught the oil lamp just as it spun off the bedside table. Ned could barely see through the cloud of dust that swirled around them. The last thing he wanted was a trail of oil leading right to them. Luckily it was daylight and the lamp wasn't lit. As the horrible sounds subsided, he held his breath, waiting for the next crash— the last one—as their haven disintegrated. He couldn't see out the door to the hall anymore, but the bedroom remained intact.

So far.

Fila's breath was coming in short pants. He wondered how much time they had left; would the rest of the building collapse in a minute? An hour?

They had to get out of here. Fast.

Chapter Nineteen

"ARE YOU OKAY?" Ned asked.

Fila got to her feet shakily. "Yes." Splintered lumber filled the hallway. Without him asking, she approached the doorway and shook her head. "It's blocked." Blocked under tons of wreckage. The hall gone, the living room gone. The kitchen, where she'd stood just moments ago—destroyed. She was shaking as she turned back to face him.

"We'll have to go out the window." Ned threw back the covers.

"Our coats—"

"Forget the coats. The rest of this place could go any second. Hand me my crutches."

She set the lamp down and did so, hovering around him as he got up. As they made their way to the window, Fila scooped up their duffel bags. "It'll only take a second to throw them out the window," she said when he glared at her.

"That second could be our last." But when they reached the generous window, he helped her open it, pushed out the screen and tossed the luggage out in a matter of moments. "You next."

"What about you?" The beams above their head groaned, silencing them both.

"Get out the damn window." Ned held back the curtain as best he could. Since the room was at ground level, it was nothing to Fila to climb up and over the sill. Ned was a different matter. He handed her the crutches, sat carefully on the sill and pulled his good leg up and over.

"I'm here," Fila said, bracing herself under his shoulders. "Just pull back as carefully as you—"

The remainder of the roof gave way with an enormous groan. Fila shrieked and hauled back on Ned. He pitched out of the window backward, bowled her over and landed on top of her. "Sonofa—" Ned writhed in pain on the cold ground as Fila fought her way out from underneath him. Wasting no time, she gripped under his arms and pulled with all her might.

Even in his pain, Ned seemed to know what she was trying to do. He kicked with his good leg, pushing against the frozen ground, helping her move him clear of the remaining cabin walls, in case they should give, too.

When they were clear, Fila dropped him and Ned didn't protest. They were both too busy gasping for breath. Ned was as pale as the snow soaking through the slippers she'd put on when she'd last taken off her boots. One look at the cabin told her they'd barely escaped with their lives.

"Now what do we do?" She peered around them frantically. The cold was already seeping through her clothes. She had to get Ned up before he was soaked to the bone. His torn sweatpants flapped in the freezing breeze, exposing his leg to the elements.

"We have to get to the Fitzgeralds. The neighbor's

place," he went on, seeing her bafflement.

"Where is it?" She looked around her at the thick woods and the truck still upside down near the driveway.

"About seven miles up that lane."

SEVEN MILES.

How the hell was he going to walk seven miles through the snow, on crutches, with a broken leg—barefoot? Already his feet, hands and ass were going numb, a strange counterpart to the fire burning where the break had occurred. Waves of pain washed through him at uneven intervals, making his stomach uncertain. He pushed down his nausea as Fila rushed forward to drag their luggage farther away from the devastated cabin and quickly rummaged through the bags, bringing up handfuls of clothes.

"We have to stay warm and dry, no matter what we do. That's the most important thing." She pulled out several shirts and sweaters for him. Ned knew she was right and he quickly sat up to don them, grimacing at the pain, even as she found more layers for herself.

"You came prepared," he grunted. He watched her swathe herself in several long-sleeved T-shirts, a couple of sweaters and a fleece.

"I was cold all the time back in the village." She rummaged further in her bag and pulled out a pair of men's house slippers. "I found these in the closet in my room. I was going to give you a lecture about not wearing them at home instead of your muddy boots."

He took them from her. "My mom gave them to me last Christmas. I never wear these things."

"You'll wear them now."

He shrugged. "Sure, but they'll soak through in a couple of minutes."

She shook her toiletries out of several plastic shopping bags. When she caught him looking, she blushed. "I don't have your little pretty zipper bags," she said defensively. "I didn't even have a suitcase before Autumn gave me this one. Didn't have anything to put in it before she bought me clothes."

"I know. What are those for?"

She pulled out two brightly colored hair ties and brought everything over to him. "Put on two pairs of dry socks, the slippers, and then wrap the bags around your feet and fasten them with the hair ties. Hurry. You're getting wet and it's getting colder."

She was right; the morning's icy rain had turned to snow. It was past noon and darkness fell early this far north. He didn't relish the idea of hiking that snowy, slippery track in the dark. He'd be lucky if he made it.

"What about your feet?" He pulled the socks onto his good foot first. He couldn't reach the foot on his broken leg. The one that still ached like a wild thing from his fall. Thank goodness Fila had splinted it tightly, otherwise he'd probably have busted it all over again.

"I'm looking." She searched through both bags and found his shaving kit. She dumped its contents into his duffel bag and held the small vinyl fabric case up to her foot. "That's one." A further search revealed nothing else of consequence. She shrugged. "I'll have to use my extra shirts. If I keep switching them I'll keep fairly dry. I have a few pairs of socks. It'll have to do."

"Take one of my bags."

"No. You're on crutches. You have to stay dry and

warm. I'll be fine."

Before he could protest further, she grabbed up the extra socks, slipper and bag and did up his other foot, catching the ends of his torn sweat pant leg in the wrapping in an attempt to keep his leg as warm as possible. Ned wanted to argue, but he was too busy fighting back more oaths at the pain as she gently manipulated his leg.

After Fila rigged up her own feet, she quickly emptied the contents of her duffel bag into Ned's, zipped it up and hooked the strap over her shoulder. "Let's get you on your feet," she said, handing him his crutches. It was harder this time than it had been back in the living room. The ground was slick with icy snow, his leg ached from the fall, and the cold air was quickly leeching away his strength. Once he was up, she helped him turn in the right direction. "Lead the way. If you slip I'll try to catch you."

Ned grimaced at the thought of falling on Fila again. He was surprised he hadn't hurt her the first time. With one last look over his shoulder at the devastated cabin, he set off through the snow, choosing his way carefully through the drifts and ruts, setting down first the crutches, then swinging his feet, testing his footing and doing it all over again. They picked their way around the upside-down truck and up the driveway to the dirt lane. The climb nearly drained Ned of all his strength. The main track was little better than the driveway, but at least it wasn't as steep. It was still knee deep in snow, however, and Ned had to lift the crutches up like wings between steps to place them down again ahead of him. It was slow going, and hard work. Soon he was sweating under his layers. When he thought he couldn't go any farther, he looked back the way they'd come. He could still see the truck and the destroyed cabin. His heart was pounding from the exertion. His thigh was on fire with pain.

They'd made it a quarter of a mile.

FILA WAS ALL too familiar with frostbite. She'd seen many cases during her winters in the Hindu Kush mountains. The white spots that indicated the first signs of damage. The blackened fingertips and noses. Its effects were devastating. Fila pressed her lips together and slogged on. She didn't have frostbite. Yet. When the cold in her toes on her right foot got unbearable, she swapped out the current garment wrapped around it for a new one, using hair ties to secure it. As long as they kept moving, she'd be fine.

Her left foot was faring better in its nylon shaving kit bag. It too was secured with hair ties looped around her foot. She thanked goodness she'd packed a whole new package of them.

Ned's crutch skidded, he wavered and she rushed to brace him up before he fell. His weight landed heavily against her shoulder and she strained to keep upright, barely staying on her own feet.

"Thanks," he grunted, the pain all too evident in his voice.

"Do you need to stop?"

"No." He kept moving, but slowly. Fila had begun to fear they'd never make it before the sun went down. When they'd set out she'd been sure they'd make it easily—they had hours before they had to worry about darkness, but as their progress slowed, the sun's inexorable descent toward the horizon seemed to speed up.

As they trudged on, the quietness began to wear on

Fila's nerves. The weight of the gray sky and burdened trees pressed down upon her heart until she wanted to give up. She knew this feeling all too well from her time in Afghanistan. The urge to lie down and never get up again. The urge to give in.

She fought against it, not just for herself but for Ned, who had to be in a world of pain. He didn't complain, didn't lie down and give up. He kept going and going, long past what any normal man could bear. If he could be so brave, she could too.

"It's a shame about that lunch you were cooking."

Fila smiled and was shocked to find she still could. "Are you hungry?"

"Damn hungry."

"Will there be food at your neighbor's house?"

"I hope so. Should be. Fitzgerald would have stocked up for an entire winter." They slogged on. Fila reflected that the snow was preferable to the morning's freezing rain.

Barely.

"I'm sorry," Ned said after a long pause broken only by the crunch of their feet and his crutches in the snow. "I shouldn't have asked you to come. You could be safe and warm at Autumn's house right now."

It was hard to picture the great room at the Cruz ranch. There would be a roaring fire in the fireplace. Food on the table. Friends gathered around, like usual. Fila sighed—she'd put up with as large a crowd as could squeeze in the place if only it meant they'd be out of the cold. "If I wasn't here, you'd probably still be lying in that truck. Dead."

"I know. I appreciate all you've done. You're a hell of a woman."

She didn't know about that, but she liked hearing it. A

hell of a woman.

"I mean it, Fila. How many people could do what you've done? Survive ten years as a captive. Figure out a way to escape. Stand up to a bunch of killers. And now this. Most women would have given up. But you're not most women."

"We should rest." His praise made her uncomfortable. If she was such a brave person, why did she spend her days holed up in an empty cabin? Why didn't she jump at the chance to run a restaurant? "I need to switch my foot wrap again." Ned made his way over to a large tree near the side of the track and leaned heavily against it.

"If I sit, I'll never stand up again," he said and rested while she worked. "You know, it used to be when you went to Fourth of July get-togethers there'd be a set of old guys sitting around talking shit about the War—World War II," he explained when Fila shot him a questioning look. "There were a few old geezers who actually went, and others who'd grown up listening to all the men talk about it back in their day. One thing always came up. Courage."

Fila changed her wrapping as fast as she could, realizing she had only a few more items of dry clothing to use. As she listened to Ned talk, she decided she'd have to use them sparingly—if she ran out, she'd be in trouble.

"The thing about courage is, it doesn't feel good in the moment."

Fila slowed what she was doing.

"Heroes aren't people who are somehow unafraid in a crisis—heroes are the people who feel afraid and still do what needs to be done." Ned watched her finish up. "I heard that over and over again when I was growing up, but I didn't get it. Not until recently."

"What happened recently?" She stood up, ready to go again.

"I met you." He made his way over to her in the middle of the snowy road. Took her hand and squeezed it, leaning heavily on his crutches. "This is going to sound all wrong, but when men fake bravery, I guess I'm as easy to fool as the next person. I just assume they don't feel fear. But when I saw you—just a slip of a thing—and I heard all that you'd done"—he shrugged—"I knew you had to have been afraid while you did it. But you did it anyway. That's my definition of brave." He dropped a kiss on top of her head and turned to keep going.

Fila stood still for a moment, warmed by what he'd said—by his understanding. Now she had a word for when she felt sick to her stomach, tied up in knots, ready to faint.

Brave.

She bit back a smile as tears clouded her eyes again.

She hated being brave.

Too bad she didn't have a choice.

They slogged on for what seemed like an eternity, until her toes went past burning with the cold, to numb, to simply not there anymore. She didn't know how she was staying on her feet. Didn't know how Ned had remained upright for so long, either.

"How much farther?" she gasped at one point.

"I'd say we're a bit over halfway there."

Halfway there. Fila wanted to hang her head and cry. It would be different if she were on her own. She could run for it and reach safety and warmth sooner. She could find boots or—

Ned must have had the same thought. "Fila, you need to go ahead. Break into the house, find something for your feet and mine. Get coats, a flashlight. Then come back for me. I'm slowing you down too much."

The idea appalled her. "What if you slip? What if—"

He turned her way. "This isn't a game. We could die out here. You could get frostbite. Heck, we both could. We might have already." He sagged down on his crutches. "Honestly, I don't see any other way."

"How do I get in?"

"However you need to. Fitzgerald won't care. Break a window. Anything. His house isn't visible from the road, though. Watch for a wooden fence. You'll see the gate across his driveway. Open it and follow the driveway down and you'll find the house."

She evaluated the proposition quickly. Dusk was already falling. Temperatures were going down. Neither she nor Ned were dressed for the weather. She could be back in less than an hour if she hurried on alone.

She would definitely hurry.

"Okay."

"That's my girl." Ned straightened. "I'll keep going, nice and slow. That'll keep me warm until you come back. Go fast, but be careful. We don't want both of us laid out."

She nodded. Hesitated. Suddenly she hated to be alone.

"Come here," Ned said softly.

She did so and he cupped her jaw with his hand. "It's going to be all right. I promise. Remember how brave you are." He kissed her until she sighed against him. She didn't pull away. She knew it was safe to kiss Ned. She was alone in a snowy wilderness with the man, but she wasn't in Afghanistan. There were no armed terrorists, no gossiping village women, no one at all to disturb them. As the seconds passed, his kiss deepened, and he slid his lips over hers until she thought she could lose herself for good in his arms. When he pulled away, Fila clung to him in wonder. He smoothed her hair back from her forehead. "Come back soon, you hear?"

She nodded and scampered away, racing down the lane into the thickening dusk.

Chapter Twenty

NOW THAT FILA was gone, Ned gave voice to the groans he'd been suppressing as he moved. Every step hurt like daggers through his skin. He wondered if he was damaging his leg by working it like this, but he didn't see an alternative—other than to freeze to death.

There was no reason Fila couldn't make it to Fitzgerald's house and bring back warmer clothing and footwear, at the least, in time to save him from permanent damage. He'd still have to make the rest of this painful journey but at least he wouldn't lose any toes. As the shadows lengthened and the night drew in, however, he began to worry about what would happen if Fila lost the track. Even if she kept to it, she might not see the fence in the darkness—especially in the falling snow. Surely the driveway would be visible, but she was tired and cold. Maybe she'd lose her way.

Ned picked up the pace, visions of Fila wandering the woods without shoes filling his brain. When his crutch hit a patch of ice under the snow it slid straight out from under him. He wavered for a moment, still balanced on the other one, before it snapped and he keeled over. He cried out with the pain of impact.

And groaned when he realized he couldn't get up again.

FILA RAN FOR as long as she could, but as the dusk turned to true darkness she realized she needed to pay close attention to the sides of the road to spot the driveway into Fitzgerald's cabin. She watched for the wooden fence Ned had told her about, trudging quickly through the snow, not bothering to change the wrapping around her foot anymore, but as the remainder of the daylight leached out of the forest, her fear came back.

Had she already passed the driveway? How many miles had she come in her headlong rush? Surely she should have seen it by now.

She told herself she'd walk for fifteen more minutes before she turned back, but then she realized she had no way to judge the passage of time. She began to count, but as her footsteps increased their pace, so did her counting. She slowed down again. Lost her place. Started over.

Gave up.

She began to think she'd be walking this path forever and ever. Back and forth, through the dark and cold, her feet numbing until she could barely stumble forward.

The pure darkness surrounding her reminded her of the mountain village she'd left behind with its absence of electricity. You could look out from the mountain and see nothing but blackness all around you. When the winter winds howled and the snow drifted up she'd felt like she'd been alone in an alien world. Once, after a particularly hard day, she'd nearly convinced herself that was the truth. She'd stood outside the compound where she lived and stared up at the stars searching for an answer there.

She'd gotten one, too. A tiny light—no bigger than a star—traveling in a straight line across the sky. A satellite, just like the ones she'd seen while stargazing at home with her parents. If satellites were real, then technology was real. If technology was real, then the United States was real. After that she searched the night skies for satellites whenever the occasion arose. They comforted her a little. They promised her that home still existed.

Fila realized with a start that she'd been so busy in the last few hours that she hadn't thought once about not fitting in or being afraid of people. All she'd done were the things she needed to do. The thought made her feel stronger. Ned was right—she was brave.

There.

Fila rushed forward. There was the wooden fence. She followed it swiftly until she came to a gap where a blank track of snow led away into the distance. Spotted the open gate. This had to be Fitzgerald's driveway. She set off carefully down the sloped track toward even deeper shadows. At least the expanse of snow that marked the drive made it easy to follow through the woods. Several minutes later, she rounded a bend and saw the squat, square shape of a cabin up ahead.

Fila's heart pounded in thankfulness and she rushed forward. She tried the doors first, found they were locked and broke the lowest window she could find. Clambering in through it, she threw down the duffel bag, felt her way down a hall to the kitchen and peered through the shadows until she found what she was looking for.

A box of matches.

She struck one with a shaking hand, located an oil lamp

like the one at Ned's family's cabin and lit it. In its bright rays, she breathed easier. She'd done the hard part. She'd reached the cabin. She could gather supplies and go back to help Ned. They were safe.

Only Ned wasn't safe; not yet. She set to work quickly, hunting for the things they needed. Back near the door she found several pairs of boots and set aside one pair for herself and another for Ned. The hall closet held several rugged winter coats. She pulled out two of them, along with mittens and hats. In a bedroom she found socks and a flashlight. Back in the kitchen she found packets of crackers which she stuffed in the pockets of one of the overcoats.

Ripping off the ridiculous footwear she sported, she chafed her toes until they tingled and burned, pulled on clean socks, shoved her feet into a pair of boots that were several sizes too big, pulled them out and layered on more socks, then tried again. She finally let herself back out the door, with the gear for Ned bundled into a cloth shopping bag, when she spied the best find of all—a plastic toboggan with a rope handle resting against a porch railing. She dropped her bundle onto it and set off back up the driveway toward the road, her heart soaring as she tugged the sled along behind her. Now she could pull Ned back here if need be. They'd be warm and fed and dry in no time.

As the minutes passed, she kept her pace strong, expecting to catch sight of Ned at any moment. While he couldn't have covered the ground anywhere near as quickly as she did, he must have made some progress—especially given the time she'd spent inside the house finding the supplies. When her journey stretched out and he didn't appear staggering through the snow on his crutches, she began to worry. With each passing minute, that worry grew. Had he run out of steam? Hurt himself again? Had he been attacked by a wild animal? She began to wish she'd thought to look for a gun.

The minutes ticked past as the cold, dark forest enveloped her. Her footsteps made small crunching sounds through the frozen snow as she walked. A slight, icy breeze blew through the rattling tree limbs, startling her now and then. She couldn't see or hear any sign that she was anything but alone in these woods.

When she finally spotted him, a dark, still shape against the white snow, Fila rushed forward with a cry, dropping the lead rope to the toboggan. "Ned! Ned—" He was icy cold to the touch, but a pulse still beat at his throat. She scrambled to retrieve the sled and load him onto it, knowing that getting him warm was more important in this moment than not jostling his leg. She slid the second pair of boots straight over his feet, leaving the one on his hurt leg entirely undone, and piled both overcoats over him, knowing the exertion of pulling him would soon keep her warm.

She turned to face the long road home and nearly wept at the thought of retracing her steps. It would take ages to pull him to safety up and down the rises of the unplowed road. And then what?

Whatever it took to keep him alive until the Mathesons came and brought them home.

A SERIES OF bumps and jolts woke Ned and he cursed thickly at the stabs of pain in his leg. The break seemed to burn from the inside out. The rest of him shook helplessly with a cold that had seeped all the way to his bones.

"I'll get the fire going. You'll be warm soon." He rec- ognized the voice—Fila's—but couldn't answer her over the chattering of his teeth. He had no idea where he was, but they were inside—that was a ceiling above him, not tree boughs or open sky.

So why was it so damned cold?

Fila heaped something soft and warm over him, but not warm enough. Shudders consumed him. His throat ached with every swallow. His head ached almost as much as his leg, his lips were parched, and objects in the room around him seemed far away and close together all at once.

"Water?" His voice was thin and rough. She raced away. Came back. Tilted his head and lifted the glass to his lips. Most of its contents spilled over his chin but he got a taste down—not enough to soothe his raw, painful throat, though. What on earth had he done to himself?

He'd been on his back like this before—in another cab- in. He searched his memory and dredged up the accident, his broken leg and the time he'd spent with Fila at his family's place.

The cave-in.

Ned tried to sit up. Fila stopped him. "We're okay now. We made it to Fitzgerald's house."

Ned sank back. Tried to remember how they'd gotten here. They'd walked part of the way, then Fila had gone ahead. Then…

He couldn't recall what came next.

At least they'd made it to shelter. If they'd spent the night outside they would have been done for.

Cool fingers touched his cheek, then his forehead. "You're burning up." Fila chafed her hands, then pressed them to his skin again. Gave a small intake of breath. "Your leg. Maybe it's infected?"

Covers shifted. She tugged down the loose sweatpants he wore over the splint. Ned groaned.

Another gasp. Fila let the breath out slowly. "You've rebroken it. I'll have to set it again."

Her words didn't make sense. Ned's world had diminished into a small circle of his aching head and the sharp, stabbing pain in his leg. Waves of nausea washed over him. He wanted to curl up, but he couldn't move his body that way. He wanted to thrash, but every jostle of his leg threatened to send him unconscious. He was dimly aware of Fila racing off again and returning several minutes later. She fiddled with the splint on his leg and he nearly howled with pain, his breath coming in great, shuddering gasps.

"Ned? Can you hear me?"

"Hnnhhh." He still couldn't form any words. She held the glass to his lips again and he drank greedily, then swore and sputtered as the liquid burned a path down his throat. Alcohol.

"Drink more. It's the only thing I have to dull the pain."

Ned tried to avert his mouth but she was relentless and he did drink more. The liquid pooled inside him, warming his throat, his stomach, his limbs. His concentration slipped. He struggled awake again when she dragged the toboggan he still lay on toward the archway between the living room and the kitchen. When she got him into position, she maneuvered the plastic sled out from underneath him. "What the hell?" he slurred.

"It's the only thing I can tie you to." She tugged him close to the decorative post that defined one side of the entryway into the kitchen and Ned's gaze darkened around the edges as she hauled him upright to sit against it. Fila went to fetch something else, came back again, and began to wrap rope around his chest and under his armpits. After several long moments, he realized she was wrapping it around the post, too.

She was tying him to it.

Why?

Pain swirled around him as she tightened the rope, until he was held so snugly against the pillar he could hardly move. "What're…y'doin?"

"I'm sorry," she said, crouching down beside him. "I have to do this. Otherwise, I don't know what will happen."

"What?" He could barely form the word. Could barely follow what she said.

She moved away from him down toward his feet, and wrapped her fingers around his ankle. In one quick movement she wrenched his leg straight.

Ned howled and passed out cold.

Again.

FILA JUST MADE it to the toilet before she was violently ill. Luckily, there wasn't much in her stomach to dispose of, and as soon as the nausea passed, she returned to Ned, re-splinting his leg quickly. She untied him, brought him back near the woodstove that was finally throwing some heat, and made as comfortable a pallet for him on the floor as she could. She heaped him with blankets and comforters and touched her hand to his brow. He was burning with fever, which scared her more than she wanted to admit. If an infection had set in at the break, she was in way over her head. She had no idea what to do to stop it.

First things first, she would search the cabin for medical supplies, food and anything else that might help. From the things Ned had said, Fitzgerald lived here year-round. He must have stockpiles of provisions that the Matheson cabin didn't contain.

A quick run-through of the house found it amply stocked with food, oil for the lamps, and other household goods. The back porch covered a large pile of firewood and she could see more under a shed roof at the end of the backyard. She found a first aid kit in the bathroom, but it only contained the usual things. The medicine cabinet revealed some pain reliever, for which she was grateful, but no stockpile of antibiotics.

She didn't find a phone, either. Ned had mentioned his neighbor had a satellite phone he used for emergencies, but he must have taken it with him when he decamped. It certainly wasn't in the house. Once she'd searched everywhere she could think of, and checked on Ned again, Fila decided food was the next priority. When Ned woke up, she needed to make him eat. Canned soup would work for the short term, she decided, but when she found dried beans in the kitchen pantry and onions in a cold storage room in the basement of the cabin, she decided to start a homemade soup for later. She ate some of the canned soup herself without relish. She knew she had to keep her strength up through the coming days until someone came to rescue them, but the food was tasteless as it crossed her lips.

Ned could get very ill if he had an infection. Untreated, the wound could fester until it sent poison through his bloodstream and finally killed him. Fila's chin wobbled and a tear slipped down her cheek. Surely someone would come for them soon. Wouldn't they?

Maybe not soon enough. This was only their second night here and Ned's father expected them to be gone for at least four days. That meant two more nights before someone came after them. She moved back into the living room to be closer to Ned. Touched his cheek again. She didn't want to lose this interesting, infuriating man now that she'd just found him. She didn't want to lose this friend who understood her better than all the others.

"Ned," she whispered softly as she stroked a hand over his cheek again. She bent over and pressed a kiss against the side of his mouth.

Chapter Twenty-One

NED'S EYES FLUTTERED open in time to see Fila withdraw. He felt like he'd been hammered with a blunt instrument all over his body. His tongue was thick and his throat hurt worse than if it had been attacked with sandpaper. But the pain in his leg has lessened to a dull roar. "Fila?"

"I'm here. You have to rest."

"Water?"

She held a glass to his lips and he prayed it wasn't whiskey this time. Then thought maybe it would be better if it was. Cold, clear water quenched his thirst a little, but it didn't soothe the pain.

"Throat's sore."

She frowned and peered at him. "You have a fever. Can you swallow some food?"

Ned nodded. "Think so."

She soon returned with soup, giving him a spoonful at a time. He swallowed it as best he could until his stomach threatened to rebel. When she gave him two pain reliever pills, he managed to choke them down with more water. Then he lay back and fought to keep his stomach from sending it all back up again.

"Bad." He wanted to say they'd gotten themselves into a bad spot. She seemed to understand.

"It's nearly nine o'clock. Two more nights until your family comes. We can do it."

Ned figured he should tell her his family might wait a day or two more—he was known for going off on his own, so they might think he was staying away voluntarily—but he couldn't form the words and besides, what was the use? They'd either come or they wouldn't.

He drifted back into sleep.

THE MATHESONS WOULD come in two more days, wouldn't they?

Maybe not. Ned was very independent. The Mathesons knew he was capable. They knew there'd be no cell phone reception at the cabin. They wouldn't worry about him if he was a day or two late. Would they worry about her? Or would they think the two of them were having so much fun off on their own…

Fila couldn't trace that thought to its end. If it was only a matter of being rescued because they'd flipped their truck they could wait here for weeks—there was plenty of food and fuel for the woodstove.

Ned wouldn't last for weeks, though. He wasn't just hurt—now he was sick, too. What if his fever climbed higher? What if the infection got worse?

Her fears increased as the night drew on and Ned began to shiver. His face shone with sweat but he jerked with violent shudders until she ran her hand up and down his arm and whispered soothing words. His fever was so high she was afraid to pile on any more blankets. Her voice and presence seemed to calm him, however. After a long moment's hesitation, she slipped under the covers next to him and pressed herself close along his side.

"It'll be all right," she whispered near his ear. "You're okay, Ned. It'll be okay."

She wasn't sure how long she murmured to him. This close to the man, she could feel every muscle in his arm, see every contour of his jaw. Everything about him was so masculine, his features so much more pronounced than her own. She allowed herself to touch him gently. To stroke his arm and run her fingers over the stubble on his jaw. She traced the curve of his ear. And, when she was sure he wouldn't wake, pressed her lips to his shoulder. Kissed him.

There was something primal about being so close to a man. Exploring his body. The contours of his muscles and the rise and fall of his chest as he breathed fascinated her. As the night wrapped them round in darkness, punctuated only by the light of the fire in the woodstove, Fila felt a kinship to all the women who'd gone before her, fearing for their loved ones, wrapping their arms around them, hoping the hours would hurry along to bring dawn around again.

He had to be all right. He had to get better. She'd give him one day. If his health didn't improve, she'd walk the eighteen miles back out to the highway. She'd do whatever it took to save his life.

HE'D NEVER FELT so bad and so good all at the same time. Ned woke to find his entire body shaking with cold. His head still pounded and a sickening throb pulsed in his thigh. At the same time something soft and warm and womanly pressed up against his left side, clinging to his arm, her face snuggled against his bicep.

Fila. Sharing his bed.

He would have laughed at his predicament if his throat didn't hurt so bad. Hurt, sick, in worse shape than he'd ever been in his life. Incapable of making a pass at the sweet woman at his side. The woman he wanted more than anything.

The woman who had been afraid of him only days before.

Had she been cold during the night, to snuggle in with him? Or had she thought he required her presence? Probably the latter, if he knew Fila. He shifted and she woke, her head lifting, brown eyes widening when she saw him looking back at her. She scrambled up and he immediately missed the comfort she'd given him.

"Are you better?" She pressed a hand to his forehead. Frowned. "You're still too hot."

"Can you blame me?" His words came out slurred. His throat was thick and swollen, tender as a newborn's skin. Did he have strep? That would just be his luck. Poor Fila. He'd meant to keep her warm and snug as a bug while he shoveled the roof of his family's cabin. Now she'd been put through the wringer to care for him.

She didn't answer. Instead, she pulled back the blankets and exposed his leg. Her fingers were soft and cool against his skin and she bit her lip as she examined the splint. "I think your leg is set correctly."

He had a moment's memory of being tied to the post. "That's some bedside manner you have. I think I passed out."

"You did pass out. A good thing, too." Still, she was frowning as she set his covers back to rights. "I don't know why you have a fever. Your leg doesn't look like it's infected."

"Maybe I'm just sick."

She plumped more pillows under his head, brought him some soup—homemade this time, he noted, even though his throat was so sore it burned on the way down. He made himself swallow several spoonfuls then shook his head when she tried to give him another one. "Can't eat."

"You have to."

"Not hungry."

That made her frown more. She gave him more pain medicine. Pulled his covers up to his chin.

"Read?" he muttered. He needed something to hold on to as the edges of his vision blurred dim again. He wanted to hear her voice.

She disappeared and returned some minutes later. "I found a cowboy book."

"Western." His lips barely moved. His eyes were closing as much as he fought against it. He was sick, he realized dimly. Really sick.

"Riders of the Dawn." She read the title. The author's name stumped her but she sounded it out. "Loo-is Lah-moor."

"Louis L'Amour." Ned opened his eyes again as he pronounced the name. Even he knew that author. A western was good.

Fila started reading, her unusual cadence making L'Amour's plain spoken characters sound vaguely foreign. The action started right away and he'd be damned if the hero didn't propose to the heroine on the very first page.

Smart man. Although the word *propose* wasn't quite right for what the hero did—more like he declared his intentions to have her for a wife and then took off on his horse.

Ned had never thought to do that. As he drifted off again, he wondered if he ought to give it a try.

Chapter Twenty-Two

FILA WAS ALL too aware that Ned was drifting in and out of consciousness as she struggled through the hard-bitten prose of the western. Many of the words were slang and unfamiliar, but she appreciated the fast pace and audacious courting style of the hero. The poor heroine didn't stand a chance.

She wasn't sure if it was good or bad for Ned to sleep so much. She heated up soup for him regularly and fed him a few spoonfuls every hour or so, forcing herself to take some nourishment at the same time.

The hours crept by slowly and her worry grew as Ned's periods of unconsciousness grew longer. He still woke up from time to time, but when he did his movements were restless, his eyes overbright.

"Love the sound of your voice," he drawled once in a moment of clarity. He moved his hand, touched hers and smiled. "Love the feel of you." He drifted off once more.

As morning shifted to afternoon, and then the afternoon waned into night, Fila's worry shifted to outright fear. Ned had begun to cough in great spasms that rocked his body and made him writhe in pain. This wasn't about his leg anymore; he must have caught the flu while they were back at Chance Creek and now it had settled into his lungs. With the onset of evening, Ned's breathing grew labored. Was pneumonia setting in? What should she do now?

She ransacked the kitchen cupboards and prepared a ginger tea with cayenne pepper, but Ned just spluttered and spit it out when she tried to spoon it into his mouth. He couldn't seem to swallow anything anymore. She'd seen people die of pneumonia in the village, coughing and gasping for air—giving up at the last. Ned wasn't going to go like that. Not if she could help it.

A sound outside had her whirling around to peer through the window into the gathering gloom. The wind had picked up again and the trees tossed and turned against the darkening sky. The sound hadn't come from them, though. It had been sharp and loud.

Like a dog's bark.

Could it be wolves? The thought made her shiver. They were safe enough in the house—she'd blocked up the window she had broken soon after she'd made it back with Ned, but if she had to hike out for help she didn't like the idea that wild beasts roamed these woods. Thank God they hadn't run into any while walking here.

The sound came again, two short barks that sounded like any dog back in the Afghan village. She pressed her face against the glass, saw movement near the back shed, but couldn't make anything out in the gathering gloom.

What would a dog be doing so far away from anyone else? Was someone else staying in one of the hunting cabins farther down this road?

No, that didn't make sense. The snow on the road in hadn't been marked by new tire treads. Maybe she was overwrought. Hearing things.

The barking came again. A shape bounded into the yard and Fila jerked back, then pressed her forehead against the glass again to see better.

Definitely not a wolf! The dog's coat was a tannish-yellow, like she'd imagined Buck's in *The Call of the Wild*. And the animal was little—just a puppy. Fila straightened and nearly laughed at the absurdity of such a creature frolicking in the snow outside. It raced right up to the house, scrabbled up the steps to the back porch and stood under the window she looked out from, leaping up and wagging its tail furiously.

Where had it come from? A puppy this small couldn't have run eighteen miles from the highway through all that snow. She watched out the window to see if a person would follow it. Maybe the dog's owner would have a phone!

She rushed to the back door, slid back the deadbolt and pushed it open. The puppy bounded straight for her, its delight in discovering her all too evident. She bent down to catch it in her arms and laughed aloud when it washed her face with its tongue.

"Who are you, little one?" The puppy wriggled in her arms. After one last, long look into the night, Fila backed into the kitchen and shut and locked the door behind her. Maybe the puppy had gotten away from its owners and somehow made its way here. She remembered seeing dog food and dog dishes in the pantry when she'd searched it earlier. She scooped some into a bowl for the puppy and filled a dish with water, too. Judging by the way the dog attacked it, he was hungry.

Worry niggled at Fila as she watched him eat. Something didn't add up here. Where was this dog's owner? Why didn't the animal look worse for wear if it had come so far on its own? Was there someone out there in the night? Someone to help her get Ned to safety? If so, what were they doing on this lonely road so far from any town?

Clamping down on her fears, she prepared another bowl of soup for Ned and brought it into the living room, carrying the oil lamp with her to dispel the darkness in the room. She set the lantern on the floor, reached down and touched Ned's forehead.

Still much too warm.

"Your friend doesn't look so good to me."

Fila straightened up and screamed.

Chapter Twenty-Three

NED SHUDDERED AWAKE again, feeling like he was clawing through layers of cotton to get to open air. Every breath seared his lungs and he wondered if the fire had leaped from the stove and sent its smoke straight down his throat. Fila was talking in a strange, high-pitched voice. Someone else was here. Someone he couldn't turn his head far enough to see. Something small and furry scurried around the room in tight circles—some kind of animal. It bounded closer. A puppy. He groaned aloud when it ran right over his legs.

"We need help. We need to get him to a doctor. Will you help us?" Fila was nearly begging.

"Depends on what's in it for me." The voice was low. Male. Surly. Ned's instincts flared—he didn't like the sound of that voice at all. It wasn't his father or one of his brothers. Wasn't Fitzgerald or his son, either. Who the hell was in the house with them?

"What can it possibly depend on? He's very sick. We have to get him help right now." The puppy ran past again, thankfully avoiding his legs this time. It circled the man, sat down and whined.

"I can see that. I also see a very pretty girl who's all alone twenty miles from nowhere. I haven't had a pretty girl at hand for a long time. A very long time."

Ned grunted with exertion as he tried to raise his head. An instant later a man's face appeared above him. Sharp, wild-eyed. Hungry looking.

Trouble.

Ned struggled, trying to sit up. He needed to get a handle on this situation. Needed to help Fila, who faced the man bravely, although her fear was plain to see.

"Better stay still, friend." The stranger looked him over. "You're weak as a baby. You put up a fight and you'll just get hurt."

"Leave her... alone." The words were barely a whisper—a testament to how ill he'd become. Ned closed his eyes. This couldn't be happening to him, not now. He was supposed to be protecting Fila. Supposed to help her overcome her fears. The puppy trotted over to him again. Licked his face.

"Dell likes you," the man said and moved away again. "But then Dell likes everyone."

"Will you help us?" Fila pressed.

"Don't get your panties in a knot, sister. I'm hungry. First you can feed me. Then I bet we can come to some arrangement."

ALL FILA COULD think to do was to throw herself on this stranger's mercy, even if every instinct she had told her to cut and run. There was something about him that went beyond his rough mannerisms. Something in his eyes that wasn't quite right. Still, he had no cause to hurt them and he was her only hope. She had no idea what he was doing out in this freezing night so far from the highway. As far as she could tell he didn't have a vehicle, but maybe he'd left it back up on the road. He was dressed better than they'd been, in modern cold-weather gear, and he carried a backpack, but the pack wasn't full. Perhaps he'd set out well-supplied but had eaten through his rations. Where had he been going, though?

"Are you hiking a trail?" It made no sense, but none of this did. Maybe if she could get him talking she could figure out a way to get him on their side.

"No, sister. I'm not hiking a trail." The man laughed at the idea.

"Do you have a car?"

He shot her a hard look. "I saw your lights. Figured you'd have some grub. A man's gotta eat. He gets lonely, too."

He hadn't answered her question and she didn't like the look in his eyes, the way he sized her up and down like her Taliban captors had done when considering who she should marry. His gaze was too familiar. It lingered on her body in ways even a western woman would find offensive. She bustled into the kitchen, not knowing what else to do. "What would you like me to cook?"

"Something smells good already. What've you got?" He crowded into the kitchen after her, making the space feel too small. She took a bowl from the cupboard, aware of his gaze raking her again, and filled it with the bean soup she'd kept simmering all day. Adding a spoon, she handed it to him.

He took it, moved to the small table and took a chair. "What the hell is a girl like you doing all the way out here with Romeo, anyway?"

"Shoveling snow off the cabin roof." She kept busy at the stove, turning up the heat under the soup and stirring it.

"This one?"

She shook her head. "Ours is down the road."

"The one that collapsed. I didn't think anyone would make it alive out of that."

She shrugged her shoulders.

"So, if this isn't your cabin, then you must have broken in. Not very neighborly of you."

She fought to keep her voice steady. "We know the owner. We will pay him back for the damage." She set her spoon down. The time had come to try to plead their case. "We can pay you for your help, too. All I want is to get my friend to safety. He's very sick. You can have whatever you want. Just help me help my friend."

"Anything I want, huh? I wonder if you really mean that."

Fila stiffened at his tone, recognizing the implied threat. She was helpless here. So was Ned. If the man meant to do her harm, she didn't know how to stop him.

"Give me some more of that." He held out his bowl, forcing her to cross the kitchen to him to take it from his hands. Just as she reached for it, he pulled it back, then laughed at her reaction. "Take it easy, just having fun with you." He offered it again. Pulled it out of her reach at the last minute. Just as she was ready to give up, he shoved it into her hands. Turning her back on him to fetch the soup, her skin crawled knowing he was watching her. The man didn't mean to help them, she knew that now. No sane person would play jokes when someone was dying in the other room.

"I think I'll take you up on your offer," he said when she placed the filled bowl in front of him. "I think I'll take whatever I want." He spoke slowly, emphasizing each word. "Don't you try to stop me, either, if you know what's good for you. Your friend there can't help you. I'll be surprised if he lasts the night. You can help him all you want in the morning, if he's still alive. I'll be long gone. After I've had my fill." His tone told her he meant more than the food she was preparing. "'Course, you may not be in such good shape yourself by then. Guess we'll see."

Her hands began to tremble and Fila fought not to drop the stirring spoon she'd taken up again. He was right. There was very little she could do against a grown man who was determined to hurt her. But she had to try. Here the law was on her side, at least. If she could stop this man—if she could conquer him—the law would back her up in a way it would never do in Afghanistan.

In a flash she picked up the pot of steaming soup, whirled around and threw it at him. The man leaped sideways, knocking his chair to the floor. The soup spattered his clothes, the pot bounced off the table, but missed him.

He was on her in an instant, wrenching her arms behind her back and clutching both her wrists in one hand. He tore a tea towel to shreds with his teeth, wrapped a strip around her wrists and bound them tightly. Fila fought back, balling her hands into fists as he tied them—straining hard to make sure there'd be some slack in the ties when she relaxed them later. When he threw her to the floor, her forehead hit the tiles and pain blossomed around her temple. She curled into a ball, bracing for whatever happened next.

"Guess I'll have to cook for myself." The man began to clatter around the kitchen and pantry, rummaging through the shelves until he found what he wanted. Fila didn't fool herself into thinking she was safe. She'd had her chance and she'd blown it. Now there'd be hell to pay.

IF HE COULD just inch a little farther to the right. Ned groaned with the exertion. Just like the stranger said, he was as weak as a baby and it hurt to think, let alone to breathe. There was nothing he could do about what was going on in the kitchen. All he could do was arm himself and hope the stranger came close enough at some point for him to do some damage.

He heard Fila's shriek just as his hand finally closed around a piece of firewood. This wasn't one of the large split logs that he couldn't have hefted right now if he tried. It was a section of a branch about a foot and a half long and two inches thick. Heavy as a club. He tucked it under his blankets wishing he had his hunting rifle, or better yet—his pistol. That man was going to hurt Fila. It was only a matter of how much.

He heard a struggle in the kitchen and then something heavy dropped to the floor. He could picture in his mind's eye what had happened. Fila had concocted some scheme or other. The stranger had foiled it. Had overpowered her and probably tied her hands. That thump had been her body crashing down. From the sounds of things, the man had decided to eat his dinner anyway. That gave Ned a little time. He scanned the room for other weapons, found none. His fingers closed around the length of wood again. *Come on*, he thought at the stranger. *Come close. Let me give you exactly what you deserve.*

THE HEAVY MEAL seemed to mellow the stranger out slightly. He sat at the table and picked his teeth, his feet stuck out at angles. "Damn, woman. I'm almost too tired to fuck you."

Fila lay on her side facing the man, her wrists tied behind her. A tear slid down her cheek, but she continued to twist her hands, making use of the slack in the fabric. Add to that the natural stretch in the strip of towel and she was close to getting free again. But then what? If she got loose he'd just hit her again. Why hadn't she waited until she was closer to the man before throwing the soup? Why had she botched her best chance? She knew what he meant to do. Raping her was only half of it. Neither she nor Ned would be alive to see the morning.

Maybe it was just Fate catching up to her. She should have been dead ten years ago when the Taliban shot her parents. She'd been living on borrowed time ever since. But Ned was a young man—he had his whole life ahead of him. He had family who loved him, friends, a ranch. He couldn't die like this. Not at the hands of this man.

She shifted to cover the movement of her arms and watched the puppy bound up to the man and put its paws up on his lap.

"What do you think, Dell? Is it time for us to have some fun?"

The puppy simply gamboled around. It was far too young for him to have trained it. The knot around her wrist loosened slightly and she quickly pulled the end out of it and felt the whole wrapping shift. Blood returned to her hands, making her fingers tingle. Fila wanted to tear her bindings free once and for all, but decided to wait. Her only chance lay in surprising her captor. And doing a better job of it than she'd done last time.

"Let's go check on your friend before we get this party started."

Rough hands gripped her arms and yanked her upright. She kept her wrists carefully together, her fingers holding her bindings tight. Her head spun and a warm trickle slid down her cheek as she found her feet. Blood. The man shoved her ahead of him through the archway into the living room where Ned lay senseless on the floor in front of the woodstove where she'd left him. She was grateful he was unconscious. The less he knew about what transpired, the better, since there was nothing he could do to stop the man.

"Maybe he's dead already." The man sounded disappointed. "What's wrong with him anyway?"

"Pneumonia. It's highly contagious." She wished the illness would jump bodies and strike the man dead right now.

He nudged Ned with the toe of his boot. "Hey, buddy. You awake?"

Stay silent, Fila prayed, but he didn't. Ned groaned and shifted. Whispered something.

"What's that?"

Ned said it again, but Fila couldn't make out his words. The man shoved her onto the sofa where she flopped like a ragdoll. She kicked and heaved herself until she was sitting upright in time to see the stranger kneel down and bend over Ned's body. Her fingers worked at the ties until she was completely free of them.

"Asshole!" Ned said at the same time he whipped a length of wood out from under his covers, and came up on one elbow to bash the man over the head with it. The man seized his arm and the club flew across the room, nearly striking the puppy, who had settled down with a sigh a moment earlier. It leaped to its feet and barked as the man punched Ned in the face. Ned howled in pain. Fila saw her chance. She leapt from the couch and snatched the log up off the floor, the puppy dancing all around her. It barked and yipped and scrambled right up and over Ned's prone body. The stranger swore at it, batted it away. Taking advantage of his distraction, Fila lifted the club over her head and smashed it down on the man's skull. Raised it again and swung it like a baseball bat to knock him off of Ned's legs. She raised it again. Brought it down. Each time it hit him with a satisfying smack. Each time the man shuddered, struggled to rise and sank down again when the log connected with his head.

She pulled up a fourth time and slammed it down. That was for her parents, shot dead before her eyes. Lifted it and swung it down. That was for her years of loneliness. Up and down. For the times she'd been beaten. Up, down. For the times she'd feared for her life. Up. Down. For the years she'd lost. Up—

"Fila. Fila!" Ned croaked, eyes wide, propped on his elbows, fighting for breath. "You'll kill him!" The puppy stood crouched behind him barking again and again.

She turned on them wild-eyed. Did he think she cared? They'd never shown her mercy. None of them. And he expected it of her? She lifted the club again.

"Fila—look at me!"

She missed, swinging around at the last second.

He held out a hand to her, gasping in pain, but refusing to lie back down. One look at his burning eyes and pleading expression and she came back to herself. She took in the man puddled at her feet. The bulk of him wrapped in a ball like a child. He was unmoving. Covered in blood.

Blood she'd shed.

Fila dropped the club. Swayed. The puppy whined but stayed by Ned's side.

"Fila." Ned tried to move to her, but couldn't. He lay panting, tangled in the blankets she'd covered him with earlier. "It's okay, honey. You're okay." He lurched to a sitting position, his breathing rough, his words even rougher. "Come here."

She shook her head, the enormity of what she'd done overwhelming her. She'd nearly killed a man. Maybe she had.

"Fila. It isn't over yet. He could wake up again."

She stared at Ned, barely comprehending his words. Wake up? The man wasn't even breathing.

Was he?

She inched forward, hardly daring to breathe herself. Placed her fingers in front of the man's face. His breath feathered over them. Shallow, but definitely there.

He was still alive and if he woke—when he woke—he'd want to kill them more than he had before.

She glanced at the branch she'd dropped.

"No," Ned said. "That way isn't for you. Find the rope you used to tie me to the post."

After a long moment she did what he said. Ned was right—she wasn't a killer.

But the thread that separated her from one was as thin as gossamer.

Chapter Twenty-Four

HE WAS DYING.

Ned could feel the pneumonia taking hold deep in his lungs in a way that left him coughing and gasping to breathe. Chances were he'd make it through another day or two—long enough for someone to rescue them—but he was getting close to a line that once crossed would be hard to come back from. If delirium took him again, Fila would be alone with a murderer. From the look of the bloody gash on the back of the man's head, he wasn't the only one walking side by side with death in this cabin.

He didn't say so to Fila, but he knew she knew it too. For the thousandth time he cursed his stupidity for ever bringing her here. The idea that he could protect her—help her—seemed truly laughable. He'd become a shell of himself. Weak, hurt, sick—dying. And Fila had been put through the wringer again.

The worst of it was he'd been nothing but a burden to her. Fila—scared, traumatized kidnap victim—had had to save his life. Several times now. She'd probably hate him for bringing her here. She'd probably run away as fast as she could the minute they made it back to Chance Creek.

If they ever made it to Chance Creek. Maybe he'd just die and save her the trouble of having to run.

He coughed long and hard, the searing pain in his lungs almost worse than the pain in his leg. This is what he'd come to. The sum of his worth. He was helpless. Useless.

Good for nothing.

"Tie him up tight," he said to Fila. "Use all the rope you have." The puppy licked his hand and he tried to pet it. "Good dog," he told it. It licked him again.

Fila took his advice and trussed the stranger to the pillar up like a pig on a spit.

Now all they could do was wait. Half a night lay ahead of them, then a full day and another night before they could begin to look for a rescue. He prayed to God for the first time in years that his family would question his absence—especially given Fila was with him.

The adrenaline that had enabled him to move and speak was fast leaving his system, rendering him aching and struggling to breathe once more. He closed his eyes just for a moment.

And slipped into sleep.

SHE'D BEATEN A man within an inch of his life.

She'd become the very kind of monster she'd fled from Afghanistan to escape.

What would her Taliban captors think now? Is this what they'd wanted all along? To turn her into a killer and set her loose among her own people?

As the seconds ticked by, the house was silent except for Ned's labored breathing and the softer inhalations and exhalations of the killer tied to the post near the kitchen.

She wanted to drag him outside and leave him in the dark and cold to die, but then she'd truly be a monster and there'd be no coming home after that.

All she'd wanted to do was protect Ned. When the man had leaned over him, fist raised, her vision had blurred and her mind had sharpened to a single point. He had to die. She'd acted on that impulse, saved her friend, but nearly taken a life.

What kind of woman was she?

She knelt next to Ned and smoothed his blond hair away from his handsome face, trying to remember who she'd been before she went to Afghanistan.

Before they'd twisted her into this caricature of a woman she was today.

Once upon a time she'd loved to sing. She had no training, other than the school choir, but she sang all the time—in her bedroom along to the songs on the radio, at school with her friends, in the shower, when she walked in the neighborhood.

She'd rarely sung in the last ten years. And then only to whisper the Afghan songs along with the others, so as not to draw attention to herself.

The old Fila sang. The new Fila was silent.

She had once loved bright colors, too—oranges and pinks and lime greens that set off her dark hair to perfection. She'd dressed like a peacock, her mother used to say, but she could get away with it in a manner her friends couldn't. Dressed in faded castoffs and a covering burka in the village, she'd wanted merely to blend in. Now she chose practical clothes. Muted clothes.

The old Fila gloried in color. The new Fila preferred beige.

Most of all, once she had loved life in all its permutations. She loved people, dogs, cats, lizards. She loved catching fireflies and letting them go. She chased butterflies, watched birds through binoculars. Her curiosity about the living world made her days a bright parade.

If it has fur it will follow Fila home, her father used to say, and he was right. She'd rescued several stray cats. She often wondered what became of them when her family disappeared. In the village, pets had a purpose, and none of them belonged to her. She had no food to give them. Nothing to call her own.

The old Fila loved animals. The new Fila…

She dug her fingers into the folds of the comforter she was smoothing over Ned. The puppy lifted its head from where it had rested it on Ned's shoulder. She reached over to pet him, shyly. She still loved animals. That hadn't changed just because she'd been stolen by the Taliban.

She still loved color, too. Even if she didn't have the courage to wear it. Yet.

She still loved music. Singing. Even if she didn't dare to open her mouth and sing along. The Taliban had made her afraid, but they hadn't changed her. Not at the core.

Not where it counted.

She straightened, taking in Ned's prone form and that of his assailant on the other side of the room. She would have fought to protect a friend like Ned just as hard before she'd ever boarded a plane to Afghanistan. The Taliban hadn't made her into a monster. She'd always come to the defense of those she loved.

No one had changed her. She was still Fila Sahar. Singer. Lover of beauty. Lover of life. Protector of her friends.

A tear leaked down her cheek. Then another. And another until she couldn't staunch the flood. But these weren't the hysterical tears she'd cried when she'd first come home, still overwhelmed with terror. These were tears of letting go—of the pain, of the fear, of the years she lost, of the family that was gone forever.

As she cried herself empty, she realized that starting over might be as painful as leaving it all behind had been. She knew what she loved, she knew what was important to her, but she had no idea how to take up the threads she had dropped a decade ago and weave them into a brand new life.

The only thing she did know was that she couldn't stop trying—not when she'd come this far.

Chapter Twenty-Five

A NOISE AT ONCE familiar and wholly out of place woke Ned. Opening his eyes he saw light spilling into the cabin. The fire in the stove was low and the air around his face was cold. The rest of him was heaped with blankets.

He took a breath and winced at the rattle his lungs made. The air seared his throat and he fought against the urge to cough, knowing he'd only jostle his leg and bring himself more pain. Still, the noise held him awake. Tense. He tried to sit up.

Failed.

Fila lay beside him curled in a ball, only a single woolen blanket pulled around her. He cursed the stubbornness that must have kept her from joining him under the covers. He frowned. What was that bruising on her forehead?

The rest of the night's events flooded his mind.

Ned sat up this time, groaning with the pain in his thigh and his throat. He was dizzy from lack of food and water. His head felt too big and his throat too thick.

Across the room, a man stared back at him, his gaze so full of hatred Ned blinked. The would-be rapist was awake too, but trussed up so tightly he couldn't move. Fila had gagged him. Ned applauded her inwardly for that choice.

Finally, he placed the sound and his heart leapt. "Fila!" He reached out and touched her arm. She jolted awake, on her knees in an instant. "It's okay. You're safe. I think someone's here."

She hesitated, cocked her head, then sprang to her feet and crossed the room, her step stuttering when she took in the venomous glare of the killer she'd defeated the night before.

She continued her path until she reached the front window. "It is someone! They're plowing the road! It's Jake!"

Ned let out a long breath. He met the gaze of the trussed up man across the room as Fila nearly danced to the front door. "Looks like the cavalry's arrived."

The man grunted and struggled against the ropes.

Several minutes later, Jake was inside, stamping off the snow from his boots and pulling Fila into a rough hug. "Am I glad to see you two! When I got to the cabin and saw your truck and the state of the place—I thought you were dead for sure. I couldn't see hide nor hair of either of you in the wreckage, though... what the hell?" Jake took in the man bound to the post and looked from Ned to Fila. His eyebrows rose as he took in Fila's bruised and scraped forehead and Ned shivering on the floor near the stove. "I finally noticed your footsteps," he continued in a more subdued tone. "They led me here." He turned back to the man on the floor. "I've already got an ambulance coming. Should I call the police?"

"If you can get reception."

"I borrowed a satellite phone from Ethan to bring

along. It's out in the truck."

"Go get it. He's not going anywhere."

Jake faced the man. "I guess you're Oliver Handel." At Ned's surprised look, he added, "He's why I'm here. We heard about the jailbreak on the news. Heard he was heading this way. Figured someone better give you a head's up, just in case. To tell you the truth I thought it was a fool's errand Dad made up to interfere with you and Fila."

"I'm damn glad you came."

FILA HEATED UP soup for all of them while they waited for the ambulance to arrive. Ned filled Jake in on the details in a voice too low for her to make out. She was glad she couldn't hear. The last thing she wanted was to relive the last three days. Her hands shook as she opened the can and spooned out its contents into a pot, but she felt more peaceful than she had in weeks. Months.

Years, maybe.

She had decided that when she returned home she would think more about the girl she once was and the woman she now wanted to be. Ned was right; she couldn't let the Taliban win by remaining caught in their web of fear. They couldn't touch her now. That time was past.

Now she needed to create a new life. A life in which she stood on her own two feet. A life which included a restaurant, a lot of friends, and a man she loved.

She looked up when Jake entered the room and got out three bowls and spoons.

"Thank you," he said, coming to lean against the kitchen counter. "For saving my brother's life. Several times."

She shrugged, not knowing what to say. She spooned

out the soup and passed him two of the bowls. The puppy trailed in and sniffed around its food bowl. Fila moved to refill it automatically. She wondered where Handel had found Dell. Had he stolen him along the way? Would they have to give him back? She hoped not.

"Ned says you're a hell of a lot braver than we've given you credit for. He says we have to stop babying you and start treating you like the woman you are. I think he's right." He leaned closer. "And for what it's worth, I think my brother's in love with you. I hope you don't throw that away because of what those people did to you, or because of my father."

Fila felt a blush creeping up her cheeks as she put the bag of dog food away. Ned was in love with her? Good. Because she was in love with him, too.

Jake waited for her to answer, and when she didn't he chuckled. "Well, I guess things won't change overnight, but I think you'll find they're different now. People will know how strong you are. There's a place for you in Chance Creek, you know. You just have to find it."

She nodded, thinking of the restaurant, and a smile lifted the corner of her mouth. Maybe she already had.

Chapter Twenty-Six

ONCE THE AMBULANCE and police arrived, there was a hustle and bustle of questions and logistics. In the end, Jake accompanied Fila to the police station in Libby to give her statement, taking the puppy along in the truck. Several hours later they were able to meet up with Ned again at the hospital, where his leg had been properly cared for and a brand new cast put on.

"The doctor commended you on your handiwork," Ned told her. His voice was still rough and his breathing labored, but he'd started an antibiotic drip. "He said my leg will knit up fine since you did a good job setting it."

"What about the pneumonia?"

"A few days on antibiotics will do the trick. I'm supposed to take it easy for a little while." He made a face. "Guess Luke will get his shot at running things."

Jake snorted. "Like anyone other than Dad ever runs things."

Fila held her tongue. She'd seen the way Holt consulted Ned when he was supposed to be in charge. She wondered if he'd do the same with Luke. "You should follow your doctor's orders so you get well as fast as you can."

"I'll be back on horseback before the snow melts. Or so he says. We'll start those riding lessons then."

Fila smiled at the thought, but a pang of sadness filled her. Where would she be when the snow melted? Now that the danger was over, she remembered Holt's dislike of her. Was there some way to change that, or would she have to leave the Double-Bar-K? The thought of not living with Ned anymore made her chest hurt.

She and Jake stayed several nights in town in a motel that accepted pets, until Ned was released with strict instructions to take his antibiotics religiously and stay off his leg. The long ride home in Jake's truck wasn't comfortable for him, especially with Buck, as Ned had renamed the puppy, making a nuisance of himself, but they made it in the end and found the whole family gathered to greet them at the main house at the Double-Bar-K.

Once inside, Lisa gathered Ned into her arms with tears in her eyes as Buck raced around the living room, delighted to have a whole new house to explore. She hugged him fiercely, then came for Fila. "I can never repay you for saving my son. Never."

Holt helped Ned to an easy chair near the fire, and propped his leg up on an ottoman. As Lisa bundled him under comforters, all the Mathesons piled into the living room to hear their story.

"I hope I never see anything like that again," Jake said, his voice thickening with emotion. "When I pulled into the driveway and saw Ned's truck on its roof—all busted up. And then the cabin demolished…" He trailed off and Fila saw it wasn't only Lisa who had tears in her eyes.

"Fila saved my ass." Ned shifted under the pile of comforters. "More times than I'd like to admit. She pulled me out of the truck, set my leg, kept me warm and fed while she shoveled off half the roof."

"You were lucky to get out of there alive," Jake interrupted. He turned to their parents. "There's nothing left standing. Nothing."

"Fila got me out. Just in time."

Holt was uncharacteristically quiet, Fila noticed. He looked old, his face nearly as drawn as Ned's was.

"What I can't figure out is how you made it to Fitzgerald's on that leg." Jake leaned forward on the couch, bracing his elbows on his knees. The others waited for Ned's answer.

"The worst of it was not having any coats. Or shoes." Ned shook his head. "Fila wrapped baggies around my feet with her hair ties. We didn't have enough, though. One of her feet was only wrapped in a shirt. In the end she went ahead to Fitzgerald's and found a sled. She came back and dragged me the rest of the way. Good thing, too. I'd fallen and passed out."

"And then Oliver Handel found you." Luke chuckled without humor. "You're like a bad-luck magnet."

"Luke," their mother chided.

"A man with a rap sheet like Handel breaks out of jail and makes a beeline for the remote cabin where Ned's lying at death's door? That's more than your average misfortune," Luke drawled.

Fila smiled a little as the others laughed.

"How the hell did you knock him out if your leg was broken?" Morgan asked. She was perched on the arm of the chair Rob sat in.

"Didn't. Fila did that, too."

Fila drew back in her chair, wishing she could hide

from the curious glances all the others were sending her way. She was not proud of the way she'd nearly lost control and cost that man his life—even if he was planning to hurt them. That wasn't the person she wanted to be.

"So Fila dragged you from a car, set your leg—"

"Twice," Ned interrupted Luke.

"Shoveled the roof, dragged you from a collapsing building, got your sorry ass seven miles down the road to safety, fixed you up again, and beat off a would-be killer?" Luke sat back. "That's a hell of a weekend, Fila."

Once again everyone turned her way.

"That's a hell of a thing you did for my family," Lisa said, more softly. "A hell of a thing to save my son not once, but three times."

"More," Ned said firmly.

"Young lady," Holt said, his rusty voice piercing through the others in the room. Fila waited, holding her breath, for his pronouncement. Here's where Holt would kick her out again. "That was a hell of a thing indeed. Thank you." He got to his feet and walked slowly—unsteadily—from the room.

"Excuse me," Lisa said and hurried after him.

In the quiet they left behind, the brothers exchanged a look.

"Told you it would work out okay," Jake said.

Ned's laugh sounded more like a grunt of pain.

SINCE NED COULDN'T easily negotiate the stairs to his bedroom, his brothers helped move the furniture in his cabin and brought his bed down from his bedroom to the living room for the duration. Once everyone had filed out the door and gone home, Fila turned to him, overcome with relief again that they'd made it home.

He moved to her swiftly, leaned on his crutches and pulled her into his arms. "I know. We're safe now, honey. Everything's going to be okay."

She leaned against him, content to let him bear her weight even though she knew she should be urging him to rest. Ned had been through so much.

But she had been through so much too. And his arms felt good around her—strong, comforting. Alive. She realized she hadn't been sure if they'd make it out alive.

"Come to bed." Ned took her hand and tugged it gently, moving backward toward the newly set up bed. They'd drawn the curtains over all the first floor windows and dimmed the lights, but a fire still crackled in the hearth.

"With you? But—"

"I don't want to be alone. Do you?"

She drew in a shaky breath. "No."

"I won't push my luck." He planted a kiss on her jaw just in front of her ear. "I'd be afraid to."

A shiver ran through her at the touch of his lips. She let him lead her to the bed where she sat and watched him strip down awkwardly to the flannel pajama pants he wore. He hesitated, his hands on the waistband. "I'll keep these on for now," he said finally.

Fila felt a stab of disappointment, then a surge of shock at her own reaction. The shock lasted only a moment. She'd chosen life and love over fear of any kind—even of a man's body. This was Ned—her Ned. The man she loved with all her heart. The man she'd nearly lost. She refused to risk losing another moment with him. Not one more moment.

He awkwardly climbed between the sheets. "Come here."

She didn't join him. Instead she pulled the sweater she wore up and over her head, then began to unbutton her blouse. Ned struggled into a sitting position to watch. After a moment, he said, "Are you sure?"

She nodded.

When the buttons were undone, she shed the shirt on the ground and lifted her hands behind her to undo the clasp of her bra.

"Fila," Ned breathed, his gaze never leaving her. She expected to feel fear, but she didn't. Instead, she longed to get it off—to be bare in front of Ned—to allow him to see her.

She wanted to be seen. She wanted him looking at her.

She made short work of the clasp. Threw the bra to the floor.

"Fila." Ned leaned forward. "Come here."

She didn't join him. Instead she undid her belt, undid the button of her jeans and lowered the zipper. She slid them down over her hips slowly, feeling Ned's gaze burning over her skin. When she hooked a finger under the waistband of her panties, Ned's breath hitched. With a twitch of her hands they fell to the floor.

Ned reached for her again and this time she went to him, climbing under the sheet he held up for her, carefully snuggling in next to him as he lay down so as not to hurt his leg. His hands slid over her bare skin and she tingled all over, wanting more. He pulled her close until her nipples grazed his chest and they both moaned. Fila found herself pressing kisses under his chin, down his neck, onto his chest, his coarse hair tickling her face. She ran her fingers over his bicep, tracing his muscles and then circled his shoulder, feeling the strength coiled within him.

"God, Fila—you feel—"

She cut off his words with a kiss on his mouth and an instant later he'd swept her closer and was kissing her back. He cut off after a few short moments with a curse. "Damn cast. I want to roll all around this bed with you." He kissed her gently. "We'll have to take it easy tonight."

She was okay with that, although the desire burning through her body made her want to throw herself at him— made her want him to touch every part of her at once.

As if hearing her unspoken wish, Ned dipped his head and traced a kiss slowly over the mound of one breast. She sighed, arching her back to meet him, loving the feel of his lips on her skin. He did it again, then trailed his mouth down to take in one nipple. Fila gasped at this new sensation, closing her eyes when his tongue began to do delicious, wicked things.

"You are so beautiful," he breathed a moment later when he pulled back, before leaning down again. Fila didn't know how long the sweet torture went on. Ned's kisses, tugs and nips heating her body until she thought she'd catch fire.

She wanted him closer. She pressed along his entire length, wanting more, but not knowing what more it was that she wanted. Ned lay back against the pillows and pulled her with him until she lay half across him, unsure what to do next. He still played with her breasts, reaching up to take first one and then the other into his mouth, until she couldn't wait anymore. "Ned."

He gazed at her—read her desire in her face. "Climb up on top of me."

"Won't I hurt you?"

"No." He helped her into position, straddling his waist, and when he tugged her down on top of him, she discovered exactly what she wanted.

Ned's hardness lay between her legs and pressed against her core in a way that set her on fire all over again. She moaned at the sensation, still wanting more—still wanting to be even closer.

"Fila—are you sure?" Ned gazed up at her, waiting for her answer. She knew whatever she said would be right. Whatever she did with Ned would be right. She nodded.

"We have to use protection. Otherwise you could get pregnant."

"I don't care." The words flew out before she could even register what she'd said.

Ned's face softened in a way she had never imagined he could look. He reached up to cup her face. "I love you, you know that?"

She nodded. "I love you too."

He closed his eyes. "Fila." Opened them again. "Will you marry me?"

Would she marry him? She bent down and covered him with kisses. "Yes! Yes! Yes!"

"Ow!"

They both stilled, then Ned laughed raggedly. "You're going to be my wife?"

She nodded vigorously.

"Forever."

"Yes."

"Come here." He pulled her down into a kiss that seared her all the way to her toes. She reached down hungrily to tug at the waistband of his pajamas.

"We don't have to," he said, breaking away from the kiss for a moment. "We can take it slow."

"We. Have. To." Fila nearly growled the words. "I want to. Now." Was he really going to deny her?

"I've got protection upstairs. It's in—"

Fila growled again. "Are you going to marry me or not?"

He chuckled. "Yes."

"I want you. All of you. Right now," she begged him. "I want to know we're alive. Together."

After a long moment he said, "Okay."

NED KNEW HE should slow down. He knew he should be taking his time to tease and stir Fila's desire into a bright hot flame. He knew he should take things one step at a time. Introduce her to each stage of lovemaking carefully.

But Fila was having none of that. She frantically tugged the waist of his flannel pants down, until he took over for her and managed it himself. As it was, he was able to get his uninjured leg free from the garment, but the pants still lay wrapped around the cast on his other leg when Fila reached down tentatively and took the length of him in her hand.

Ned groaned and clutched the bedclothes, wondering how much torture he could sustain. It had been a long time since he'd been with a woman—a really long time. And he'd wanted Fila for months.

He slid his hands up her thighs to her hips, taking in the lush beauty of her. He still couldn't believe she was perched on top of him, ready to love him—ready to give him everything.

She leaned forward and braced her hands to either side of him, shifting her hips until she slid along his hardness again. Her breath was coming fast and light, and she kept moving, kept sliding over him—the tips of her nipples tracing lines of fire against his chest again and again.

His hands moved to cup her bottom and nudge her into place. He shifted until he pressed against her. He wanted to ask her again if she was ready, and at the same time didn't want to. Could he stop now? He wasn't sure.

Fila took matters into her own hands. She lifted her hips and settled down on top of him, letting out a breath in a silent, "Oh," as he slid inside a little bit and then a little more. With an expression of intense concentration, she lifted up and settled down on him again. Ned held back with every fiber of his being, not wanting to hurt her—wanting to let her call the shots.

Slowly, carefully, with movements so seductive he could barely hold himself together, Fila let him in. There was a moment of surprised pain which made Ned stop altogether, but it was only a moment before Fila began to move again. Stronger this time, more sure of herself, until he slid all the way inside her with a groan that expressed his feelings better than words ever could.

She paused until Ned searched her face to see if something was wrong. She seemed to be considering something.

"What is it?" he whispered.

She shut her eyes. "I'm feeling you."

He nearly lost control right then, but held on some more until he thought that this might be divine retribution for all of his prior sins. Then Fila began to move again. Up and down. Faster and faster, moving with an animal grace that brought him to life. Now he allowed himself to move, too. Thrusting into her as she slid down his length, slowly at first, then faster to match her pace. He was rewarded when she sped up again as well, and together they found a pleasing rhythm.

Best of all was when she lowered herself down to lie on top of him and allowed him to take control. Ned thought that no one had ever given him such a gift—the trust she showed in him let him know she'd be his forever. He was determined never to let her down.

He slowed his pace again to long, strong strokes that had her begging for more. She pressed kisses into his neck, clinging to him, murmuring words that didn't make sense but that he understood anyway. Cupping her bottom with his hands, grinding her into him as he thrust into her, he increased his pace bit by bit until he could tell she was barely holding on.

She crashed into her release with a cry of such abandon that Ned went over the edge too. Bucking against her, filling her full, crying out himself—they shuddered into a tangle of an embrace. Still breathing hard, Ned gathered her close and kissed her. He would never get enough of this. Never get enough of her.

He would never, ever let Fila go.

Chapter Twenty-Seven

"WAKE UP. I need to buy you a ring."

Fila came to with the most luxurious sense of rightness at finding herself in Ned's arms. The events of the previous night rushed into her mind and she couldn't help but smile.

"I could lie here all morning and just look at you," Ned said, tracing a finger over the contours of her face. She kissed his fingertip as it slid over her lips, then turned and snuggled closer.

Her second attempt at lovemaking went more smoothly than the first and fulfilled her in ways she hadn't dreamed possible. She felt like she was coming alive after years lying parched and forgotten in a desert. Why didn't everyone do this all the time? When she asked Ned, he laughed.

"We can try."

They did try. But as the morning went on, he finally pulled away. "I'm serious about that ring, but someone's going to have to drive us. Do you have Rose's number?"

"Yes." She fetched him her phone, feeling oh-so-wicked for prancing about the cabin naked, but she liked knowing he was watching—that it was right for him to watch.

Her fiancé.

Soon to be her husband.

She left him reluctantly while he made the call and showered and got dressed. He took his turn in the bathroom and described the clothes he wanted from his closet. As she went up and downstairs, helping him get ready for the day and whipping up a quick breakfast of cereal and toast, Fila realized this was only the beginning. She and Ned would belong together from here on in—they'd make a whole life together.

She couldn't wait.

Rose arrived and swooped Fila immediately into a big hug. "Congratulations! I'm thrilled you're going to let me help you pick out the ring!"

"But you won't spill our secret?" Ned came nearer on his crutches. "I want to announce it at Fila's dry run of the restaurant on Saturday."

"I won't spill. And I'll help you get ready for Saturday any way I can."

A half-hour later they were perusing the glass cases of Thayer's Jewelers where Rose had worked until recently. Rose had emitted a sigh of relief when they walked in and found her old boss wasn't present. "Hi, Andrea," she called. "This is Fila and Ned—they're old friends of mine."

Andrea came and handed her a set of keys. "Emory's not coming in today. Take your time."

"She lets you have the keys to the cases?" Ned asked. "Even though you don't work here anymore?"

"Only on special occasions," Rose said. "We're friends," she explained. "And I let her vent about Emory to me whenever she needs to. Which is a lot." She smiled. Fila knew that Rose's former boss had been a thorn in her side, so she understood. Rose began to point out rings she thought might suit.

Fila loved the way Ned kept a hand on her at all times during the proceedings, as if she might slip away from him if he wasn't careful. It was a far different thing than the way her captors had watched over her—it came from a place of desire, not of control.

The ring they chose in the end was both delicate and strong. A little old-fashioned, but that suited her. It made her think of the strength of traditions, while the more playful elements reminded her there was always room for change and growth.

Fila wanted to wear it home, but it needed a slight adjustment, and they'd already agreed to debut it at her restaurant's dry run. Now it was time to get busy preparing for the day when her friends would taste-test her food. Everyone had volunteered to help. She needed to make to-do lists and contact them.

The next few days flew by for Fila in a whirlwind of planning and preparation. Mia, Hannah and the women from the Cruz ranch took turns shopping with her and getting everything set up at the restaurant. Fila combed the Internet for tips on staging so many meals at once and Autumn filled her in on everything she knew about cooking for a crowd.

"When I serve my guests, I serve them all at once, like a family, though," she cautioned. "That's pretty much how it will be for your dry run, but on a normal day you'll need to know how to serve people continuously over the course of hours—that's a whole different ballgame."

Fila wished she knew someone with more experience to consult.

"What about Camila?" Mia asked her on Friday morning when they were stocking the refrigerator with the last perishable ingredients they would need for the following day. "She's got lots of experience, right?"

Fila tried to hide her reaction. Why wouldn't she consult Camila? Because Camila had set her sights on Ned? So what—she was the one about to wear his ring. Because Camila hogged everyone's attention with her outgoing ways and her winning smile? That was just petty.

Petty, but true.

Fila sighed and told herself not to be ridiculous. If she really wanted to be the star attraction of a gathering, then she needed to learn to shine. And if she didn't want all that attention, then she couldn't complain if someone else hogged it. "Okay. I'll see if she's next door."

"I didn't see lights on when we came in." But Mia trailed her to the door and over to Camila's restaurant. No one was inside, so they decided to head home for an early lunch with Ned and Luke before coming back for the remainder of the afternoon.

When they pulled into the long lane leading into the Double-Bar-K, Mia was the first to spot the car in front of Fila and Ned's cabin. "Isn't that...Camila's?" she said as they pulled in beside it.

Fila nodded, her chest tightening with suspicion. Why would Camila come here? To see her?

Or to see Ned?

She slipped out of Mia's truck and quickly dashed up the stairs to the cabin's front porch. Twisting the handle of the front door, she barged right in—

In time to see Camila spring apart from Ned and Ned scramble to throw a blanket over his legs.

He still sat propped up on the bed they'd installed in the living room. Camila was obviously flustered. So was the man who was supposed to announce their engagement tomorrow. Fury filled her in a split second.

"Fila—" Ned pushed himself up straighter. "I didn't expect you for another fifteen minutes."

"What are you doing?" Fila didn't even recognize her own voice, it was so strident.

"Nothing."

"Ned—" Camila ran her hand through her hair, smoothing it into place.

"Nothing." He shot a look at Camila. His growl reminded Fila of Holt's when he was laying down the law.

She wasn't fooled. They'd been kissing. It was plain as day. Fila backed up a step, fumbling behind her for the door. She had to get out of here—had to—

"You have to tell her." Camila turned on him. "What she's thinking is worse!"

A strange look passed between them. A knowing look.

Fila had seen enough.

She spun around, reached blindly for the handle through eyes already filling with tears. She should have known she wasn't destined for happiness. Should have known pain would follow her wherever she went.

"He's reading!" Camila shouted after her, her tone exasperated. Fila hesitated and the front door banged into her as Mia rushed in, her mouth dropping open in surprise when she saw Fila's tears.

"What's wrong?" Mia looked past Fila, her eyes widening as Camila rushed toward them, a textbook held aloft in her hand. "Duck!" Mia knocked Fila aside, sprang for Camila, and tore the book from her fingers. Camila tripped and went down hard.

"What the hell—ow!" Ned lurched from the bed and staggered toward them, his cast thumping on the hardwood floor. "Mia—what are you doing?"

Fila caught her balance and swung around to see Mia brandishing the book over Camila's head. "You saw her! She was going to hit Fila!"

The door swung open again and Luke spilled in. "Is it lunch time—hey, what's going on?"

"Your girlfriend is beating up my tutor! Get her off!" Ned bellowed.

Luke reached down and plucked Mia away from the wild-eyed Camila, who surged up after her, swearing up a blue streak in Spanish. Ned caught her arm before she could pounce on Mia.

But Fila wasn't watching Camila anymore. She was watching Ned. Replaying his words.

His tutor?

What kind of tutor?

She grabbed the book from Mia who was squirming in Luke's arms.

Elements of Literacy.

"Damn it!" Ned reached her and snatched it from her hands. Held it behind his back.

Literacy? That meant reading, right?

The truth hit her and she clapped a hand to her mouth, nearly laughing out loud at the misunderstanding. Of course Ned wouldn't want her to know he was learning to read. He wouldn't be able to admit that to anyone.

But he had to Camila.

Fila scowled. "She's teaching you to read?"

Ned frowned fiercely, but finally nodded once. "I went to the volunteer bureau. They assigned me to her." His face had turned an interesting color and she knew him well enough to understand he was pushed to the edge of his capability to keep control.

Well, so was she. "That's all she did?"

"Assigned her to do what?" Luke broke in, looking bewildered. Ned's shoulders slumped. After a moment he held up the book so Luke could read the title. Luke's eyebrows shot up.

"Huh."

Ned met her gaze. "That's all she did. I can't believe you have to ask."

She bit her lip, then relaxed and let go of the anger that had filled her. Of course Ned wasn't fooling around with Camila. She knew he was in love with her. Every touch and glance told her so. Poor Ned. He was trying to learn to read, and now four people knew—four too many, if she judged him correctly.

Filled with a sudden compassion for him, she turned on Mia and Luke.

"Neither of you will ever mention this again. Not you, either," she said to Camila. "You will teach him when I'm home, so people think you're visiting me. Understand?"

For a moment she thought Camila would argue, but in the end she only nodded. Fila turned to the other couple. "Understand?"

Mia's gaze shifted from her to Ned to Camila before dropping. She had stopped struggling. "I understand. Sorry, Camila."

"You don't need to be sorry," Camila said, taking the

book back from Ned. "Neither do you, Fila. Your instincts were right; I wanted more from Ned. I've been pretty clear about that." She met Fila's gaze directly. "You said he wasn't your boyfriend."

"He wasn't." Fila stood her ground. "But I wanted him to be. Now he is."

"Now I'm your fiancé, you mean." Ned took her hand, his grip telling her the distinction was important to him.

"You should have said something," Camila told her.

"You're right, I should have."

Camila pursed her lips, her normal animation gone. "I just want to fit in here. I want friends—a boyfriend. I want to feel like I can make a home here. I guess that's too much to ask."

"You still have your restaurant." Mia disengaged from Luke's arms. "I'm sure that's going to be a success."

"No—it isn't." She wrapped her arms across her chest. "My father found out that my uncle was loaning me money. He demanded that my uncle stop. My uncle doesn't want to split the family, so he's not sending any more. I don't have enough—I can't buy any ingredients. I can't pay next month's rent. I'm a complete failure." As her tears spilled over, Mia rushed to comfort her. Fila saw Ned and Luke exchange a look and she knew what they were thinking—only moments ago the two women had nearly come to blows.

But that was before they'd understood each other. Knowing what she did now, Fila could put aside her animosity toward Camila, too. Camila wasn't so brave after all—she was just another woman who was trying to make her way in the world. She stepped forward to hug her.

"I don't want to break up this little lovefest," Luke

drawled, "but are we ever going to have lunch?"

As NED STUMPED over to the kitchen table and sat down, his heart was beating double-time in his chest. For a minute there he thought he had lost Fila. Camila had called him to check up on his missed appointment and suggested she come over right away to make up for it. Since there was no way for him to get to town without someone else's aid—which would expose what he was up to—he said yes. He was already sick of television, sick of sitting still. He might as well have something to do.

He could tell something was bothering Camila right from the get-go, however. She'd come in, sat down on the edge of his bed, as far from him as she could get without falling off the side of it, and had taken far too long to find her place in the materials she used to teach him.

He'd waited as patiently as he could for her to spill the beans, but when she started in on the lesson, jabbing her finger at each grouping of letters she wanted him to try to decipher, he decided he'd had enough.

"What's going on?"

"Nothing." She kept her attention on the book she'd placed in the wide space between them.

"I'm not going to bite—you can move a little closer."

"Why? It wouldn't do me any good."

He hadn't understood her meaning at the time—not until Fila and Mia's dramatic entry.

Camila had been interested in him all this time, and he hadn't even noticed because his attention was squarely on Fila. He supposed he should be flattered, but all he felt was relief that Camila hadn't inadvertently run his engagement right off the rails.

He felt bad for her—new in town, broke, her family dead set against her chosen profession. Families sure did find all kinds of ways to screw with each other.

Now he watched Fila move swiftly around the kitchen, assembling a meal with Mia's help. She peppered Camila with questions and he realized that if he'd thought he'd found himself a quiet, meek wife, he was definitely mistaken. The way she'd issued orders to everyone about keeping his secret was startling, but gratifying. She'd made huge strides when it came to self-confidence.

She was finding her voice.

"CAMILA, CAN YOU give Fila any hints about how to handle a constant flow of customers?" Mia asked when they were all seated. "She knows how to serve a meal to a large number of people if they're all eating at once, but she doesn't have restaurant experience—if it's not too hard for you to talk about," she rushed to add.

"It's okay." Camila seemed resigned. "It's a matter of getting things prepped ahead of time so the final cooking takes as little time as possible. Depending on what you're serving, the dish might be almost done except one last cooking stage. Or you might have all the ingredients chopped and ready, but not be able to assemble or cook the dish until the customer places their order. I could look over your menu items and talk it through with you after lunch."

"That would be great." Fila passed her a bowl of salad.

"Why don't you two just join together?" Luke said, helping himself to three pieces of naan—another type of flatbread Fila liked to make. "You could serve Mexican-Afghan food."

Mia dropped her fork onto her plate with a clatter. "That's an awesome idea! You should totally do that!"

Fila turned to Camila and saw the same trepidation she felt mirrored in the other woman's eyes. Ned began to chuckle. "I don't think either of these ladies could share a kitchen."

"It's still a good idea. Then you wouldn't be competing for customers—you'd be sharing them," Mia said.

"More hands make lighter work," Luke said.

"You could each be in charge of your own menu items," Mia added. "There are already two stoves—what if you added some more prep space and had two of everything—maybe you could split the kitchen."

"Maybe," Fila said slowly. She tried to think it through. Now that Camila wasn't trying to impress her, she had decided she liked her a lot more. Could they work together? Did she want to? Camila certainly had a lot of experience she could learn from.

"I know!" Mia sat forward. "You can do a double test run tomorrow—both of you serve your dishes at the same time, working in the same kitchen. If it's a success, you can move forward together. If you hate it—you'll forget all about it."

"That makes sense." Fila turned to Camila. "What do you think?"

"Tomorrow?" Camila hesitated. "I have some ingredients I would need for that, but not everything—not the fresh ones."

"Give me a list," Luke said affably. "I'll pick up what you need. You can either pay me back from your restaurant earnings, or when you get a new job."

"You'd do that? Why?"

"Because that's how we roll around here," Mia said happily. "Everyone helping everyone else." She slipped her cell phone out of her back pocket. "All right—let's spread the word about this new development. Fila and Camila's Restaurant. Huh, that's kind of clunky." She chewed her lip. "Famila's. Families…"

"Familia! That means *family* in Spanish!" Camila's face fell. "But it's Fila's restaurant—and you already have a sign. You should keep your name even if we do work together."

"Fila's Familia," Mia suggested. "I like the sound of that."

"I like it too," Fila said. She did—she was beginning to feel like she had a family here in Chance Creek.

"Let's get through the test run and make up our minds later." Camila stood up. "I'd better get to work!"

"Me, too." Fila couldn't wait.

Chapter Twenty-Eight

"ARE YOU READY to tell the whole world that you're going to be Mrs. Ned Matheson?" Ned lay back in his bed and braced Fila in his new favorite position—her straddling his hips, him pressing inside her, urging her on to ecstasy.

"I didn't know I was changing my name to Ned." She laughed at his expression, then moaned when he surged inside her then drew almost all the way out. She squirmed on top of him, trying to press back down, but he held her in place.

"That's Mrs. Ned." He surged inside her with a swift stroke.

Her gasp left her unable to answer and he took advantage of the situation, thrusting into her again and again until her cries rang out through the cabin. He shouted his own release soon after, and it wasn't until they lay entwined and panting that he took the subject up again.

"Are you ready to make our announcement?"

"Yes!" Her assurance brought a smile to his face. He couldn't wait to tell everyone the news. He wanted to broadcast it to the world. Fila Sahar was marrying Ned

Matheson. As soon as possible. In fact—

He pushed himself up on his elbows. "Let's set the date."

She trailed a hand down to caress him, seeming all too interested in going for another round. It was a good thing he'd broken his leg, Ned reflected happily. Otherwise his ranch chores might get in the way of their lovemaking. They'd have to make hay while the sun shone, so to speak, since his vacation was only temporary. As he stirred to life again below the belt he thought he could put up with that for now.

When Fila was ready to concentrate on other things some time later, he brought up setting the date again. "I think we should hold the wedding soon—before you open Fila's for real. How about Valentine's Day? That's just under a month away and you're still waiting on permits and inspections, anyway. By that time you'll be just about ready to open. We'll grab a quick honeymoon, come home and get back to work."

She made a face. "I'd rather stay here in bed with you, but if I can't, that sounds perfect."

"I'll let Mom and Dad know."

"I'll take care of telling everyone else."

THE DRY RUN was both chaotic and successful—more fun than Fila could possibly have imagined, with more accidents and upsets than she could have predicted, too. While they wanted all their guests to end up in the restaurant to celebrate together, they also wanted a chance to experience what it would be like with customers coming in at staggered times. Mia had come up with the idea of having several groups of people arrive in ten minute increments. All their guests came to the counter to place their orders like normal customers and Mia rang them up at the till, although they charged no money.

They recruited Hannah and Morgan to act as servers to bring the meals out to the guests and clear away unused dishes when they were done. They'd arranged the dishes into groupings, so their customers could try small portions of several menu items at a time. Fila and Camila raced around the kitchen responding to orders and cooking as fast as they could. Camila kept up a constant stream of chatter and exclamations in Spanish as she worked, which at first threw Fila off her stride, then made her laugh until she nearly cried when she realized Camila was talking to her ingredients. She soon grew used to the noise and eventually blocked it out by humming the pop tunes she'd begun to memorize. Between Camila's talking and her snatches of songs, the kitchen was a lively place.

After everyone had been seated and served, Fila and Camila took a break and came to the front to eat with the rest of the guests. Camila slid into an empty spot next to Lisa. Fila was surprised when Holt slid out of the same booth and made his way over to where she leaned against the counter.

"The only thing I can't figure out is why you still eat the food your captors fed you. Why don't you hate it as much as you hate them?"

Fila glanced down at her plate. It contained a strange mixture of Afghan and Mexican dishes. She held up a flatbread. "This isn't Taliban food—it's Afghan food. It's my mother's food. I grew up eating it before I was ever captured. To me it means love and tenderness, not hate and violence."

"Taliban, Afghan—it's all the same."

She waved the bread. "No, it's not. Not one bit. Afghan culture is over two thousand years old. And it's a conservative culture—it's had to be—but it's not a culture of monsters. Afghans are people like you, Holt. They're born, they grow up, they live and love and they die just like we do. I didn't study much history before I was taken, but I know this much. America's story is that of the frontier—of always having room to grow. Afghanistan's story is that of occupation. By the Russians, the British, the Mongols— even the ancient Greeks. On and on for century after century. Imagine all those wars being fought in Montana. Foreign armies living among us, taking over your ranch, stealing everything you own, killing your wife and children, over and over and over again." She paused to catch her breath. "Death is right around the corner for them—all the time. Is it any wonder that a movement that turns men into warriors and codes everything else into rigid rules might seem like the answer?" She still wasn't sure if Holt was following her. What analogy would make sense to him? She wracked her brain. "If a bunch of Californians overran Chance Creek and forced everyone to eat tofu, would you refuse to ever eat steak again?"

He made a face. "Of course not!"

"Then imagine the Taliban are the Californians, forcing everyone to eat tofu. And everyone does it because they don't know what else to do. They still love steak, but they will be severely punished if they eat it—so will their families. That's what it's like for many Afghans living under Taliban control. It's not their choice. They still love their country. They still love their heritage. That doesn't mean they love the group of extremists who have taken over."

"Even if those Taliban people went away, they still wouldn't be anything like you and me." Holt crossed his arms.

Fila suppressed a smile at his inclusion of her. That was a step in the right direction even if the greater message was lost on him. "They're more like you than you think. Defensive. Angry. Always on the lookout for trouble."

Holt straightened. "I have four sons. Of course I'm on the lookout for trouble."

"They have sons, too." She waited to see if he understood.

Holt shook his head. "We're going to see different on this one. But I understand about the food. Everyone likes their mother's cooking best." He surveyed her plate. "You got any more of that bread?"

She'd take that as a victory.

NED TAPPED HIS spoon against his glass and whistled for everyone's attention. When the hubbub had died down and his father had made his way back to his table, he gestured for Fila to come join him. She placed her plate on top of the counter and threaded her way through the crowded room to stand near his chair as he pushed to his feet.

"I want to thank you for coming out and supporting Fila—and Camila—tonight." He waited until the cheers and clapping died down. "This test run is a big occasion for several reasons. All of you who know Fila know she's come a long way to reach Chance Creek, and an even longer way to cast off her past and embrace a new future." The crowd grew boisterous again. Ned took advantage of the distraction to pull out a small box from his pocket and hold it up. His mother gasped.

"There's another reason I wanted you all here tonight. A personal reason." He leaned on his crutches while he opened the box. "I asked Fila the other day if she'd marry me. She said yes." He waited a beat. "Maybe she's changed her mind." He turned to her. "What do you say? Still up for it?"

She nodded, her eyes bright with tears. Ned lifted her hand and slipped the ring on her finger.

"Good thing. 'Cause I wasn't going to let you get away."

This time the clapping and shouting went on and on so long Ned thought it would never stop. Soon the cries coalesced into a single word. "Kiss! Kiss! Kiss!" He didn't know who had started it and he didn't care. He swept Fila into his arms, leaned her back and kissed her until neither of them could breathe. When they came up for air, Mia and Camila were circling the room with glasses and champagne. He wondered how they'd procured them, but a look at Luke told him all he needed to know. As usual, his brother's gaze was latched onto Mia like a homing beacon. There'd be another match soon if he wasn't mistaken.

His mother's embrace wiped away all thoughts of Luke. "When is the wedding?" she cried when she finally let him and Fila go.

Ned raised his voice over the crowd again. "The wedding is Valentine's Day! I hope you'll all join us!"

"Valentine's Day! That's perfect!" Lisa hurried off again.

Ned bent down to kiss Fila. "You all right with all this?"

"More than all right. I can't wait to make a life with you."

"Damn, woman." He drew her close again. "You're already my life."

The **Cowboys of Chance Creek** series continues with **The Cowboy Earns a Bride**.

Be the first to know about Cora Seton's new releases! Sign up for her newsletter here!

Other books in the Cowboys of Chance Creek Series:

The Cowboy Inherits a Bride (Volume 0)
The Cowboy's E-Mail Order Bride (Volume 1)
The Cowboy Wins a Bride (Volume 2)
The Cowboy Imports a Bride (Volume 3)
The Cowgirl Ropes a Billionaire (Volume 4)
The Sheriff Catches a Bride (Volume 5)
The Cowboy Lassos a Bride (Volume 6)
The Cowboy Earns a Bride (Volume 8)
The Cowboy's Christmas Bride (Volume 9)

Sign up for my newsletter HERE.
www.coraseton.com/sign-up-for-my-newsletter

Read on for an excerpt of **The Cowboy Earns a Bride**.

"THAT'S CLOSE ENOUGH."

Mia Start lifted the shotgun and sighted down its length, her fingers trembling not from fear, but from the bitter cold of the early morning air. In the field of brightness created by her truck's headlights, her form-fitting, quilted, pink winter coat was the only splash of color in a quarter mile. Beyond her, the snow-covered fields and forests that lined the icy, back-country road were as black as a Montana midnight, even though it was half-past five in the morning.

"For God's sake, Mia—put down the gun." Ellis Scranton wore a formal gray wool coat over his customary suit and lifted a hand to screen his face from the truck's high beams. His Mercedes' lights were on, too, but weren't nearly as bright.

He didn't look armed.

She still didn't trust him.

"Why'd you want to meet me?" She'd been more than a little surprised to get his text late the night before and barely slept in the intervening hours. Today was Valentine's Day—hardly the time to meet with your ex. In her fantasies she'd imagined spending the day in bed with Luke Matheson, the cowboy whose spare room she currently rented.

The cowboy she'd never get to be with—because of Ellis.

She and Ellis had broken off their relationship nearly four months ago when she announced her pregnancy and he announced he'd been lying all along; he didn't love her, didn't intend to divorce his wife and didn't intend to help raise their child, either.

"We need to talk." Ellis took a step closer. Mia raised the gun half an inch.

No, they didn't. She'd moved on. It hadn't taken her long to realize she'd been nothing more than a mid-life crisis to the forty-two-year-old man. The difference in their ages had once excited her. Now it disgusted her. She didn't want him in her life—or in her baby's either.

She was struggling with the consequences of their affair. She'd moved out of her parents' home before they could learn their twenty-one-year-old daughter was dating a middle-aged man—a middle-aged *married* man. The room she rented from Luke in his cabin on the Double-Bar-K ate most of her earnings from her job at the local hardware store. Soon she'd work for her friends Fila and Camila at their brand-new restaurant, but that wouldn't involve a wage increase. She knew she should force Ellis to pay child support, but that meant keeping him involved in her baby's life. She didn't want that. She just didn't know how else she could possibly raise this child.

The worst part of the whole mess, though, was the ache of knowing she'd caused pain to another woman—another mother. She'd been so swept away by the older man's attentions, she hadn't thought about his wife's feelings at all. Ellis had told her he and Elaine were practically separated—that they didn't talk, didn't share a bed, certainly didn't make love. He'd told her he'd divorce Elaine as soon as he could. All lies. And she'd been stupid enough to believe them.

"Say what you have to say."

He lifted his hands. "Are you going to shoot me?"

She took in his tired, lined face, his thinning hair and felt a wave of revulsion, but not over his looks. It was his deception that killed her—the fact he'd even pretended to love her. If only he'd been honest, she wouldn't be in this fix.

If only she'd met Luke first.

"You're the one who asked me to meet you on a deserted road at the crack of dawn. Maybe you're the one planning to shoot me."

"Fair enough. I deserve that."

Mia narrowed her eyes. This was new. Ellis never admitted he was to blame for anything.

"I'm here to say good-bye, Mia."

She lowered the shotgun an inch. "Where are you going?"

"Wyoming. Elaine has family there." He took a deep breath. "She and I, we're going to try to make a go of it.

We'll start over somewhere new, somewhere no one knows about the way I screwed up. I owe it to her. I owe it to my children. None of them can hold their heads up in this town."

"You think I can?" She couldn't keep her resentment out of her voice. She was over him. Long over him. Yet it hurt to be the one used and discarded.

"No one knows that's my baby."

"It won't be hard for them to put two and two together. Everyone's gossiping about us seeing each other."

"All the more reason I've got to go. But that doesn't mean you can't change the story once I'm gone. Tell them what you want—you had a one-night stand with a stranger. Someone from out of town. Just don't bring me into it. I'll deny it all the way." He took a deep breath. "Look, I'm sorry, Mia. I've been an ass from start to finish. You're right to hate me. When I think about how I came in and ruined your life, I just want to… Well, I think my leaving is the best thing I can do."

A chill ran through her that had nothing to do with the weather. "Just like that? You'll leave me pregnant? Alone? I have no money, Ellis! What about the cost of the birth?"

"This should help." He held out a small white envelope.

"A couple of fifties won't get it done!" She didn't recognize her own voice. She sounded desperate, as if she wasn't over him at all. It wasn't Ellis's desire to leave that had her tied up in knots, however. It was fear. Of being destitute. Of having to give up her child. Of failing…

"It's not a couple fifties. I wouldn't do that to you, no matter how big an ass you think I am." For one moment the old Ellis was back. The confident man who'd swept her off her feet. "Just don't go and blow it all on pretty clothes and a vacation to Hawaii. Go to Matt Underwood, the accountant—you know him, right? Ask him for help when you make your decisions. It takes a lot of cash to raise a kid right. More than you know."

Anger surged through her. He was speaking to her as if she was some dumb child herself. "And this is it? I'll never see you again?"

He studied her, as if trying to decide whether she was happy or sad about that. "That's right. Never again. But you won't be alone for long. That Luke Matheson will have you married in no time and you can bank on that family. You've lived with him since December, right? With a little luck you can pass that baby off as his."

"I would never do that. I'm not a liar, like—" She stopped mid-sentence. What was the use? Ellis was leaving. She let the shotgun drop. He stepped toward her.

"You're going to be okay, Mia. Let me be okay, too."

"Fine." She tucked the firearm under her arm, strode forward and ripped the envelope from his hand. "But you keep out of my life. Don't ever come back—don't ever come looking for this child. You've given up the right to have anything to do with him."

Ellis nodded, turned his back and walked quickly to his car. The Mercedes pulled away before Mia even made it back to her truck. Sitting in the cold cab, she tore the envelope open, expecting another of Ellis's tricks. It was too thin for its contents to amount to much. A few hundred. Maybe a thousand. There was no way—

Mia stared at the cashier's check she pulled from the envelope.

Two hundred thousand dollars. Ellis had given her *two*

hundred thousand dollars. A wave of dizziness crashed over her as she realized what this meant.

Ellis was out of her life. Forever. But he'd given her the means to do what she'd known for months she'd have to do.

Raise this baby alone.

It was several long minutes before she could start the truck and pull back onto the road. As she drove down through the dark, silent country highway toward the Double-Bar-K, Mia decided she needed a cup of decaf coffee before she could face her day. She wished she could get the caffeinated kind, but she'd have to wait a few more months for that. She bypassed the ranch and headed into town.

She couldn't sort through her emotions. She was relieved Ellis was gone. She'd lived in fear of being called out for their affair for months, and she knew the minute friends and acquaintances spotted her pregnancy, they'd have a lot to say. With Ellis—and his wife and children—out of the way, the speculation would be easier to bear. Mia would carry her shame for hurting Elaine the rest of her life; she didn't need everyone in town pointing their fingers at her. She felt hopeful, too. The money he'd given her would go a long way toward raising her baby in comfort. The money brought its own problems, however. Ellis might think Luke would step in and marry her, but she knew better. No man as proud as Luke Matheson would want a pregnant bride. By giving her enough cash to move out from Luke's spare room, Ellis had unwittingly ended her brief stint in paradise.

Living with Luke had been a dream, the kind you never wanted to awake from, but she'd never slept with the cowboy—only kissed him once. It had been enough for her to be close to him. To get to see him first thing in the morning and last thing before going to bed at night. To fall asleep knowing only a bedroom wall separated them. That proximity had kept her hopes alive.

Now it was time to leave all that behind, and with Ellis's money, she didn't even have the excuse anymore that she was too poor to move.

Two hundred thousand dollars.

She wasn't poor anymore.

She parked on the street near Linda's Diner, which opened early to suit the hours of the hardworking ranchers who lived in these parts. She found a booth where she could escape notice and smiled gratefully when the waitress, Tracey Richards, poured her a cup of decaf without even being asked.

"Anything else?"

"No." Mia thanked her and took a sip of the scalding liquid. She should have known she wasn't meant for happiness. Men always caused her trouble. Ellis Scranton was only the latest example. She shook her head at the memory of a worse offender—Fred Warner—pushing down the ache of pain it caused. Warner had ruined her beauty pageant career—no great loss except that it had dashed her mother's hopes of having a beauty queen for a daughter, and ended the closeness between them long before Mia's indiscretions with Ellis did. Ellis was the root of all her current distress, though. If only she'd never met him!

No.

Mia placed a protective hand over her belly.

No, she'd never wish their relationship away. Not really. If she'd never met Ellis, she wouldn't have this baby—this baby who already meant the world to her. Yes, in a perfect world, she'd get to have Luke, too, but this wasn't a perfect world.

"Coffee and a bagel with cream cheese, please."

Mia looked up at the familiar voice and saw Inez Winter take a seat at one of the tables in the center of the diner. Inez caught her eye and quickly turned away, color staining her pale skin.

Mia looked away just as quickly. She didn't speak to Inez these days, although they'd once been good friends. Inez had been on the beauty pageant circuit, too. She'd been a contestant in Mia's last pageant, back when they were both fifteen, but she hadn't defended Mia when rumors started flying about her and Fred Warner, who was a pageant judge. Inez hadn't said a word, even though Mia had seen her slip into a supply closet with the man during one of the practice sessions—the same closet he'd tried to lure Mia into before she'd told her mother about him.

Mia bit her lip, swallowing the pain that never quite went away. Inez hadn't spoken up. None of the other girls had. It had been Mia's word against Warner's and Warner won out.

No one believed her when she told them he'd tried to kiss her—tried to touch her. Mia swallowed. The truth—the truth she'd told no one, not even her mother—was that he *had* touched her. She'd figured out pretty quickly that no one wanted to hear that. Just speaking up about Warner and saying he'd lured her into a closet was enough to start a firestorm that turned all the other contestants against her. At first, her mother though she'd lied, too. Mia had realized that if she told the whole truth—that his hands had gone all kinds of places on her body before she fought him off—everyone would hate her even more.

So she hadn't said a word.

Mia took a deep cleansing breath and sipped her coffee. All that was years ago. She wasn't a vulnerable little girl anymore. She was a woman—almost a mother. And now she had enough money to get her own place and begin a new life. She'd be strong for her son or daughter, and she'd always believe them when they told her things. She'd always protect them.

"Mia?"

Mia jerked and her coffee spilled over the side of her cup.

"Sorry. I didn't mean to startle you."

Mia looked up into Inez's serious face. "That's okay." Was Inez really talking to her? After six years of silence?

Inez took a shaky breath. "Look, there's something I should have said to you a long time ago. I want to say it now. Can I sit down?"

Mia nodded, bracing herself for more recriminations. She didn't know what she'd do if Inez dragged up the past and called her a liar again.

"Fred Warner raped me."

Mia clapped a hand to her mouth and her eyes brimmed with tears. That was the last thing she'd expected Inez to say. "Oh my God, Inez. Are you okay?"

"I'm fine." Inez blinked rapidly. "Well, actually, no—I'm not really fine, but I'm seeing a counselor and she urged me to talk to you when I told her what happened. I'm so sorry, Mia. I should've spoken up back then, but I was too scared. I didn't want anyone to know what happened."

Mia took her hand. "It's okay. I'm okay. He didn't hurt me like that."

"But he tried, didn't he?' Inez scrubbed her eyes with the heel of her hand. "And you spoke up—you told people. I wanted to thank you for that. He would've come after me again if you hadn't, I know it."

"I'm so sorry he hurt you. If I'd known—"

"You couldn't have known. And I wouldn't have brought it up now, but I can't stand the fact that you hate me—"

"I never hated you," Mia cried. "I just… missed you."

"I missed you, too."

Mia stood up, moved around the table and hugged Inez. "You don't have to miss me anymore. Thank you for being brave enough to tell me. I swear I won't breathe a word to anyone else."

Inez lifted her eyes to hers. "That's just the thing. I want you to speak up. Fred Warner—he's still judging beauty pageants."

"DID YOU GET a nice gift for that lady friend of yours, Luke?"

"I sure did, Mrs. Stone." Luke Matheson smiled at the old woman who leaned on her cane on the front porch of her small house. Bundled up in her white winter coat, hat and gloves, she looked like a grandmotherly snowman. "Got her a real pretty bracelet to go with the flowers and candy I bought her."

"That's one lucky girl. 'Course any woman would be lucky to have a man like you."

"I don't know about that." The compliment warmed

him, though, as he shoveled the last bit of snow off her walkway. She'd been one of his favorite people ever since he was just a boy and she and her husband, Thomas Stone, a hired hand, lived at the Double-Bar-K. Back in those days when life on the ranch got too much for Luke, between his brothers' scrapping and bickering and his father's legendary bouts of temper, he'd escape to the little log house on the edge of the property the Stones had rented—a house that had long since been torn down. His own mother was no slouch, but Amanda Stone kept the tidiest house Luke had ever seen. Stepping into it, sitting down at her spotless table, and being served a snack on her clean, white china was a welcome change from the chaos at home.

Amanda had always understood his need for order. Luke liked things in their place. He liked knowing what was going to happen next. He liked being prepared. His father and brothers, on the other hand, seemed to enjoy flying by the seats of their pants. Ned might keep his workshop tidy and Luke's mother might have been spot on with the ranch's accounts back when she did them, but the rest of them thrived on disorder and controversy. Sometimes Luke couldn't stand it anymore. The Stones had moved off the ranch over a decade ago and bought a modest house on the west side of town. Now that Thomas had passed away, Amanda lived there alone.

"Would you like some breakfast?"

"Not today. I'll be eating with the family. It's Ned's wedding day, you know."

"Tell him congratulations from me and get on home. You shouldn't be over here messing with my walk today of all days."

"Glad to help, Mrs. Stone—and don't you hesitate

about turning your thermostat up if you're chilly. There's enough cash in your account to see you through the winter." A few years back he'd come over to find her shivering and discovered she didn't have the funds to pay her heating bill. Since then he'd arranged to pay a deposit to each of the utility companies in advance so if she was a little short she wouldn't lose her services. He figured it was the least he could do. When she had car trouble six months ago, he'd taken the vehicle to the shop only to find the repair bill topped a thousand dollars. He told her it was a hundred and made up the difference because he knew how much independence meant to Amanda.

These days, however, that independence was getting pricey. He'd replaced a window in her kitchen that wouldn't open anymore, dealt with a foundation issue that let moisture into her basement and soon he was afraid he'd need to replace her roof.

"Say hi to Mia for me, Luke. She's such a sunny thing."

"I will. See you next week!"

He checked his watch and picked up speed as he stowed away his shovel in the shed he'd built a year ago, and got into his old truck to make the trip back to the Double-Bar-K. His engine refused to turn over the first time he turned the key. He held his breath as he turned it a second time. There, that did it. Pretty soon he'd need a new truck, too. That was going to stretch his finances.

As he drove home, however, his thoughts turned to a happier topic.

Mia.

Today was the day.

Today was the day he and Mia would stop being just friends and get on to the good stuff. It was Valentine's

Day—and his brother's wedding day. Surely that double-dose of romance, plus the gifts he intended to shower her with, would finally convince the pretty young woman that the man she was looking for was right under her nose.

He could never tell with Mia, though. Every time he thought he'd got the measure of her, she surprised him. Hell, she'd managed to keep him at arm's length for two long months now, and they were living in the same house.

He frowned as he turned into the long lane that led to his family's home. He pulled up in front of his parents' house and parked. If he couldn't move his relationship with Mia to a more romantic level soon, he wasn't sure what he would do. Living in close proximity to her was driving him wild. It was hard to concentrate when she was around—and it was doubly hard, pun intended, to sleep knowing she was right next door.

He exited his truck and made his way into the house where the smell of bacon led him straight to the dining room, where most of his family was already seated. Everyone who lived on the ranch had gathered to eat and then help set up for the wedding. He wasn't entirely surprised to see Mia's customary chair empty, however. He knew she wanted to look extra good for the wedding. He ducked into the kitchen to wash up and slid into his own seat just in time to snag the platter of pancakes from Ned's hands. If Mia didn't make it, he'd put together a plate of food and bring it to her after he ate.

"Paris."

Luke jumped when his mother, Lisa, slapped a glossy brochure down on the dining room table in front of his father, Holt. Everyone stopped eating and stared at her. Luke didn't blame them. This early in the morning the extent of the conversation at the Matheson table was generally limited to a few grunts and an order or two, although usually there wasn't such a crowd.

Luke slathered his pancakes in butter, then drenched them in syrup, but took a moment to study his family before his first bite. Lots had changed recently. Only last September all his brothers had been single. After today he'd be the only one who could claim that status.

To his right sat Jake, his oldest brother, and Jake's wife, Hannah. Married just before Christmas, Luke hardly saw them these days because they were both so busy with classes they'd just started at Montana State and their regular work—Hannah with Bella Mortimer, the local pet veterinarian, and Jake with Bella's husband, Evan Mortimer, a wealthy man with an interest in sustainable ranching.

Holt pushed the brochure out of his way. "Nnnh?" he growled.

"Paris, France," Lisa said, pushing it closer to Holt again. "That's what I want for our thirty-fifth wedding anniversary this fall. A trip to the City of Love." She sat down beside her husband and helped herself to some bacon and eggs.

"Paris sounds lovely," Morgan said from her seat next to Hannah.

Morgan had married Luke's youngest brother, Rob, back in September. Rob had partnered with Ethan Cruz from the ranch next door, and was also helping Morgan start a vineyard. Luke bet Morgan and Rob would love to travel to France to check out the wineries.

"Why the hell would you want to go to Paris?" Holt said.

Luke saw Ned and Fila exchange a look. They sat on

his side of the table, Luke closest to Holt and Fila beside him. Ned was only a year older than Luke and he and Luke had argued a lot as kids—well, as adults too, until this year. Now they found themselves agreeing about more things. He was glad Ned had found a woman like Fila to love. She'd made him a better man. She was a beauty, too, with her coffee and cream skin and waist-length hair. She was funny, too, with a dry sense of humor she expressed more and more as she gained confidence. In Luke's opinion, the couple deserved a memorable wedding day. Fila had been to hell and back when she'd spent ten years as a prisoner of the Taliban, and Ned had barely survived a recent disastrous trip to the family's hunting cabin last month that left him still healing from a broken leg.

"Come on, Holt, you old goat. You'll love Paris," Camila Torres said, helping herself to orange slices. Luke marveled that his old man put up with her sass. Somehow she'd gotten into his good graces. Maybe it was her amazing Mexican cooking—so fantastic, even Holt liked it. Or perhaps it was because she was co-owner of Fila's new restaurant and now that Fila had saved one of Holt's son's lives, any friend of hers was a friend of his.

"Who wants more bacon?" Lisa asked, passing the platter around. Luke was amazed his mother had pulled off this kind of breakfast today. He'd seen the kitchen. Every spare inch was filled with items for the wedding feast.

"All there is in Paris is foreigners." Holt took the rest of the bacon and used his elbow to push the brochure farther away.

Luke ignored the back and forth. At twenty-nine he knew better than to interfere when his parents bickered. You'd think they could call a truce for Valentine's Day—

for Ned's wedding—but his parents' marriage seemed to run on friction, and today evidently would be business as usual.

There were no roses at his mother's seat. No box of candy, either, but if he wasn't mistaken, those were new diamond earrings in her ears.

"There's delicious food and beautiful architecture—and the Louvre, too," Lisa said.

"A bunch of stuck-up pansies."

"And shopping and art galleries and monuments."

"I'd go to Paris in a minute if it meant I could stop dealing with that damn architect. He's sent over so many alternate plans it's making my head spin," Jake said. Luke knew what he meant. Holt had given Jake two hundred acres to do with as he pleased, and he and Hannah meant to build a house this summer.

Lisa smiled sympathetically at her oldest son. "Building is always such a bother, but you'll be happy this fall when you move into your new home."

"I told Evan if I was rich I'd buy his place—let him go build."

Hannah laughed. "Yeah, but he shot that idea down pretty quickly. Apparently he and Bella are having just as much trouble getting her clinic and pet shelter built as we're having with our house."

"It'll all be done by the time Holt and I fly off to Paris," Lisa assured her.

"I ain't going, and neither are you." Holt made eye contact across the length of the table with his wife for emphasis, then caught Luke's expression and fixed him with a scowl. "What're you snickering about over there?"

Luke straightened. "Nothing, Pops."

"I have a bone to pick with you."

Uh-oh. Classic Holt technique. When an argument with his wife got too hot, he'd pick a new one with a son. Luke braced himself.

"See all this folderol?" He waved at the wedding preparations. "Time for your share. I've gotten the rest of your brothers hitched, now it's your turn."

"*You've* gotten them hitched?" Lisa got up again and disappeared into the kitchen for a moment. She came back with a plate stacked high with toast. "More like they got hitched in spite of your interference."

"He can interfere away, Mom. I'm all for marriage."

Lisa sat back down in her seat. "Then what's the deal with you and Mia?"

"Yeah," Ned said. "What *is* the deal with you and Mia?"

Luke glanced at the empty chair beside him. "She's getting ready for the wedding. She should be here any minute." He hoped his family would leave things at that, but of course they didn't.

"You're living with her. Your intentions better be pure," Lisa said.

"My intentions are far from pure, but our living arrangements sure are. That's the problem." Shit. He shouldn't have said that out loud. Jake guffawed and Hannah elbowed him.

"Hush, Jake." Lisa turned to Luke. "Then Mia's smarter than I gave her credit for. It doesn't do to give away the milk for free—"

"Mom!"

"Slap a ring on her finger and she'll put out soon enough," Holt declared.

Lisa dropped her fork on her plate. "Is that why you married me, you old coot? So I'd put out?"

"I thought that's why you married me," Holt countered.

Everyone laughed, and Luke knew his parents' spat was over as quickly as it had begun.

"I bet Mia's blowing you off because of your truck. What woman in her right mind wants to ride around in that old thing?" Jake said.

"It's not his truck, it's his hat," Ned said. "He's worn the same one since fourth grade."

"It's the fact he hasn't taken her out to a single restaurant," Rob said. "Luke, face it—women don't marry cheapskates."

"Yeah, you're lucky we'll still be seen with you."

Luke rolled his eyes at their teasing, but some of the barbs hit home. He had a reputation for being cheap because he was often broke. And while that was partly his own fault—he liked a night out at the Dancing Boot as well as the next guy—it was more a result of helping Amanda Stone.

If he was smart, he'd let someone else know about the old woman's problem, but he knew what would happen next. Amanda's house and possessions would be liquidated and she'd be put in one of the state-run homes for the elderly. It was a smart solution—the right solution—but Amanda Stone was terrified of old-age homes. She'd broken down and told him about her fears one day five years ago—the day he'd found her shivering in her house. It turned out her grandmother had been institutionalized with Alzheimer's and Amanda had been the one to discover the systemic neglect she'd suffered. She was terrified it would happen to her, too. She'd sworn him to secrecy and he'd promised not to tell anyone about her difficulties in maintaining her home. At first it hadn't been hard to help her keep it up and cover a few of her costs, but now he was in over his head.

His father spoke up again. "I gave your brothers deadlines to speed things along."

"Won't work with me," Luke said, coming out of his reverie. "I'm not the one holding up the proceedings. Mia is. Beside, you won't kick me off the ranch. I'm the only extra pair of hands you've got left." It was true; Jake and Rob were too busy with their own ventures to do more than help out now and then with some of the chores, and Ned was still recovering from breaking his leg last month. That left Luke and Holt to pick up the slack.

"I'll think of something."

Lisa sighed. "You know what, old man? I think you'll just mind your own business for once."

"I will, will I?"

"Yes, you will. Because I'm going to set the deadline this time. Luke, you've got six months to convince that girl to marry you, or I'll help her move along. No, don't worry—I won't be rude. There's no sense in either of you keeping the other from meeting your true love, if you aren't meant to be together. Meanwhile, your father won't say one word about marriage during that time." She held up a hand when Holt began to sputter. "Not one word, or you'll take me to France. That's the deal. Keep quiet and we'll celebrate our thirty-fifth anniversary on the ranch. Speak your mind and we'll go to Paris." She beamed. "My money's on Paris."

"My money's on me finding another place to live,"

Luke growled, pushing back from the table. "You can't kick Mia out of my house if I want her there. Besides, I don't see what the hurry is."

Lisa became serious. "I think you will all too soon."

End of Excerpt

Read on for an excerpt of Volume 1 of
The Heroes of Chance Creek series –
The Navy SEAL's E-Mail Order Bride.

"BOYS," LIEUTENANT COMMANDER Mason Hall said, "we're going home."

He sat back in his folding chair and waited for a reaction from his brothers. The recreation hall at Bagram Airfield was as busy as always with men hunched over laptops, watching the widescreen television, or lounging in groups of three or four shooting the breeze. His brothers—three tall, broad shouldered men in uniform—stared back at him from his computer screen, the feeds from their four-way video conversation all relaying a similar reaction to his words.

Utter confusion.

"Home?" Austin was the first to speak. A Special Forces officer just a year younger than Mason, he was currently in Kabul.

"Home," Mason confirmed. "I got a letter from Great Aunt Heloise. Uncle Zeke passed away over the weekend without designating an heir. That means the ranch reverts back to her. She thinks we'll do a better job running it than Darren will." Darren, their first cousin, wasn't known for his responsible behavior and he hated ranching. Mason, on the other hand, loved it. He had missed the ranch, the cattle, the Montana sky and his family's home ever since they'd left it twelve years ago.

"She's giving Crescent Hall to us?" That was Zane, Austin's twin, a Marine currently in Kandahar. The excitement in his tone told Mason all he needed to know—Zane stilled loved the old place as much as he did. When Mason had gotten Heloise's letter, he'd had to read it more than once before he believed it. The Hall would belong to them once more—when he'd thought they'd lost it for good. Suddenly he'd felt like he could breathe fully again after so many years of holding in his anger and frustration over his uncle's behavior. The timing was perfect, too. He was due to ship stateside any day now. By April he'd be a civilian again.

Except it wasn't as easy as all that. Mason took a deep breath. "There are a few conditions."

Colt, his youngest brother, snorted. "Of course—we're talking about Heloise, aren't we? What's she up to this time?" He was an Air Force combat controller who had served both in Afghanistan and as part of the relief effort a few years back after the massive earthquake which devastated Haiti. He was currently back on United States soil in Florida, training with his unit.

Mason knew what he meant. Calling Heloise eccentric would be an understatement. In her eighties, she had definite opinions and brooked no opposition to her plans and schemes. She meant well, but as his father had always said, she was capable of leaving a swath of destruction in family affairs that rivaled Sherman's march to Atlanta.

"The first condition is that we have to stock the ranch with one hundred pair of cattle within twelve months of taking possession."

"We should be able to do that," Austin said.

"It's going to take some doing to get that ranch up and running again," Zane countered. "Zeke was already letting the place go years ago."

"You have something better to do than fix the place up when you get out?" Mason asked him. He hoped Zane understood the real question: was he in or out?

"I'm in; I'm just saying," Zane said.

Mason suppressed a smile. Zane always knew what he was thinking.

"Good luck with all that," Colt said.

"Thanks," Mason told him. He'd anticipated that inheriting the Hall wouldn't change Colt's mind about staying in the Air Force. He focused on the other two who were both already in the process of winding down their military careers. "If we're going to do this, it'll take a commitment. We're going to have to pool our funds and put our shoulders to the wheel for as long as it takes. Are you up for that?"

"I'll join you there as soon as I'm able to in June," Austin said. "It'll just be like another year in the service. I can handle that."

"I already said I'm in," Zane said. "I'll have boots on the ground in September."

Here's where it got tricky. "There's just one other thing," Mason said. "Aunt Heloise has one more requirement of each of us."

"What's that?" Austin asked when he didn't go on.

"She's worried about the lack of heirs on our side of the family. Darren has children. We don't."

"Plenty of time for that," Zane said. "We're still young, right?"

"Not according to Heloise." Mason decided to get it over and done with. "She's decided that in order for us to inherit the Hall free and clear, we each have to be married within the year. One of us has to have a child."

Stunned silence met this announcement until Colt started to laugh. "Staying in the Air Force doesn't look so bad now, does it?"

"That means you, too," Mason said.

"What? Hold up, now." Colt was startled into soberness. "I won't even live on the ranch. Why do I have to get hitched?"

"Because Heloise says it's time to stop screwing around. And she controls the land. And you know Heloise."

"How are we going to get around that?" Austin asked.

"We're not." Mason got right to the point. "We're going to find ourselves some women and we're going to marry them."

"In Afghanistan?" Zane's tone made it clear what he thought about that idea.

Tension tightened Mason's jaw. He'd known this was

going to be a messy conversation. "Online. I created an online personal ad for all of us. Each of us has a photo, a description and a reply address. A woman can get in touch with whichever of us she chooses and start a conversation. Just weed through your replies until you find the one you want."

"Are you out of your mind?" Zane peered at him through the video screen.

"I don't see what you're upset about. I'm the one who has to have a child. None of you will be out of the service in time."

"Wait a minute—I thought you just got the letter from Heloise." As usual, Austin zeroed in on the inconsistency.

"The letter came about a week ago. I didn't want to get anyone's hopes up until I checked a few things out." Mason shifted in his seat. "Heloise said the place is in rougher shape than we thought. Sounds like Zeke sold off the last of his cattle last year. We're going to have to start from scratch, and we're going to have to move fast to meet her deadline—on both counts. I did all the leg work on the online ad. All you need to do is read some e-mails, look at some photos and pick one. How hard can that be?"

"I'm beginning to think there's a reason you've been single all these years, Straightshot," Austin said. Mason winced at the use of his nickname. The men in his unit had christened him with it during his early days in the service, but as Colt said when his brothers had first heard about it, it made perfect sense. The name had little to do with his accuracy with a rifle, and everything to do with his tendency to find the shortest route from here to done on any mission he was tasked with. Regardless of what obstacles stood in his way.

Colt snickered. "Told you two it was safer to stay in the military. Mason's Matchmaking Service. It has a ring to it. I guess you've found yourself a new career, Mase."

"Stow it." Mason tapped a finger on the table. "Just because I've put the ad up doesn't mean that any of you have to make contact with the women who write you. If it doesn't work, it doesn't work. But you need to marry within the year. If you don't find a wife for yourself, I'll find one for you."

"He would, too," Austin said to the others. "You know he would."

"When does the ad go live?" Zane asked.

"It went live five days ago. You've each got several hundred responses so far. I'll forward them to you as soon as we break the call."

Austin must have leaned toward his webcam because suddenly he filled the screen. "Several hundred?"

"That's right."

Colt's laughter rang out over the line.

"Don't know what you're finding so funny, Colton," Mason said in his best imitation of their late father's voice. "You've got several hundred responses, too."

"What? I told you I was staying..."

"Read through them and answer all the likely ones. I'll be in touch in a few days to check your progress." Mason cut the call.

REGAN ANDERSON WANTED a baby. Right now. Not five years from now. Not even next year.

Right now.

And since she'd just quit her stuffy loan officer job, moved out of her overpriced one bedroom New York City apartment, and completed all her preliminary appointments, she was going to get one via the modern technology of artificial insemination.

As she raced up the three flights of steps to her tiny new studio, she took the pins out of her severe updo and let her thick, auburn hair swirl around her shoulders. By the time she reached the door, she was breathing hard. Inside, she shut and locked it behind her, tossed her briefcase and blazer on the bed which took up the lion's share of the living space, and kicked off her high heels. Her blouse and pencil skirt came next, and thirty seconds later she was down to her skivvies.

Thank God.

She was done with Town and Country Bank. Done with originating loans for people who would scrape and slave away for the next thirty years just to cling to a lousy flat near a subway stop. She was done, done, done being a cog in the wheel of a financial system she couldn't stand to be a part of anymore.

She was starting a new business. Starting a new life.

And she was starting a family, too.

Alone.

After years of looking for Mr. Right, she'd decided he simply didn't exist in New York City. So after several medical exams and consultations, she had scheduled her first round of artificial insemination for the end of April. She couldn't wait.

Meanwhile, she'd throw herself into the task of building her consulting business. She would make it her job to help non-profits assist regular people start new stores and services, buy homes that made sense, and manage their money so that they could get ahead. It might not be as lucrative as being a loan officer, but at least she'd be able to sleep at night.

She wasn't going to think about any of that right now, though. She'd survived her last day at work, survived her exit interview, survived her boss, Jack Richey, pretending to care that she was leaving. Now she was giving herself the weekend off. No work, no nothing—just forty-eight hours of rest and relaxation.

Having grabbed takeout from her favorite Thai restaurant on the way home, Regan spooned it out onto a plate and carried it to her bed. Lined with pillows, it doubled as her couch during waking hours. She sat cross-legged on top of the duvet and savored her food and her freedom. She had bought herself a nice bottle of wine to drink this weekend, figuring it might be her last for an awfully long time. She was all too aware her Chardonnay-sipping days were coming to an end. As soon as her weekend break from reality was over, she planned to spend the next ten months starting her business, while scrimping and saving every penny she could. She would have to move to a bigger apartment right before the baby was born, but given the cost of renting in the city, the temporary downgrade was worth it. She pushed all thoughts of business and the future out of her mind. Rest and relax—that was her job for now.

Two hours and two glasses of wine later, however, rest and relaxation was beginning to feel a lot like loneliness and boredom. In truth, she'd been fighting loneliness for months. She'd broken up with her last boyfriend before Christmas. Here it was March and she was still single. Two of her closest friends had gotten married and moved away in the past twelve months, Laurel to New Hampshire and Rita to New Jersey. They rarely saw each other now and when she'd jokingly mentioned the idea of going ahead and having a child without a husband the last time they'd gotten together, both women had scoffed.

"No way could I have gotten through this pregnancy without Ryan." Laurel ran a hand over her large belly. "I've felt awful the whole time."

"No way I'm going back to work." Rita's baby was six weeks old. "Thank God Alan brings in enough cash to see us through."

Regan decided not to tell them about her plans until the pregnancy was a done deal. She knew what she was getting into—she didn't need them to tell her how hard it might be. If there'd been any way for her to have a baby normally—with a man she loved—she'd have chosen that path in a heartbeat. But there didn't seem to be a man for her to love in New York. Unfortunately, keeping her secret meant it was hard to call either Rita or Laurel just to chat, and she needed someone to chat with tonight. As dusk descended on the city, Regan felt fear for the first time since making her decision to go ahead with having a child.

What if she'd made a mistake? What if her consultancy business failed? What if she became a welfare mother? What if she had to move back home?

When the thoughts and worries circling her mind grew overwhelming, she topped up her wine, opened up her laptop and clicked on a YouTube video of a cat stuck headfirst in a cereal box. Thank goodness she'd hooked up wi-fi the minute she secured the studio. Simultaneously scanning her Facebook feed, she read an update from an acquaintance named Susan who was exhibiting her art in one of the local galleries. She'd have to stop by this weekend.

She watched a couple more videos—the latest installment in a travel series she loved, and one about over-the-top weddings that made her sad. Determined to cheer up, she hopped onto Pinterest and added more images to her nursery pinboard. Sipping her wine, she checked the news, posted a question on the single parents' forum she frequented, checked her e-mail again, and then tapped a finger on the keys, wondering what to do next. The evening stretched out before her, vacant even of the work she normally took home to do over the weekend. She hadn't felt at such loose ends in years.

Pacing her tiny apartment didn't help. Nor did an attempt at unpacking more of her things. She had finished moving in just last night and boxes still lined one wall. She opened one to reveal books, took a look at her limited shelf space and packed them up again. A second box revealed her collection of vintage fans. No room for them here, either.

She stuck her iTouch into a docking station and turned up some tunes, then drained her glass, poured herself another, and flopped onto her bed. The wine was beginning to take effect—giving her a nice, soft, fuzzy feeling. It hadn't done away with her loneliness, but when she turned back to Facebook on her laptop, the images and YouTube links seemed funnier this time.

Heartened, she scrolled further down her feed until she spotted another post one of her friends had shared. It was an image of a handsome man standing ramrod straight in combat fatigues. *Hello.* He was cute. In fact, he looked like exactly the kind of man she'd always hoped she'd meet. He wasn't thin and arrogant like the up-and-coming Wall Street crowd, or paunchy and cynical like the upper-management men who hung around the bars near work. Instead he looked healthy, muscle-bound, clear-sighted, and vital. What was the post about? She clicked the link underneath it. Maybe there'd be more fantasy-fodder like this man wherever it took her.

There *was* more fantasy fodder. Regan wriggled happily. She had landed on a page that showcased four men. Brothers, she saw, looking more closely—two of them identical twins. Each one seemed to represent a different branch of the United States military. Were they models? Was this some kind of recruitment ploy?

Practical Wives Wanted read the heading at the top. Regan nearly spit out a sip of her wine. Wives Wanted? Practical ones? She considered the men again, then read more.

Looking for a change? the text went on. *Ready for a real challenge? Join four hardworking, clean living men and help bring our family's ranch back to life.*

Skills required—any or all of the following: Riding, roping, construction, animal care, roofing, farming, market gardening, cooking, cleaning, metalworking, small motor repair…

The list went on and on. Regan bit back at a laugh which quickly dissolved into giggles. Small engine repair? How very romantic. Was this supposed to be satire or was it real? It was certainly one of the most intriguing things she'd seen online in a long, long time.

Must be willing to commit to a man and the project. No weekends/no holidays/no sick days. Weaklings need not apply.

Regan snorted. It was beginning to sound like an employment ad. Good luck finding a woman to fill those conditions. She'd tried to find a suitable man for years and came up with Erik—the perennial mooch who'd finally admitted just before Christmas that he liked her old Village apartment more than he liked her. That's why she planned to get pregnant all by herself. There wasn't anyone worth marrying in the whole city. Probably the whole state. And if the men were all worthless, the women probably were, too. She reached for her wine without turning from the screen, missed, and nearly knocked over her glass. She tried again, secured the wine, drained the glass a third time and set it down again.

What she would give to find a real partner. Someone strong, both physically and emotionally. An equal in intelligence and heart. A real man.

But those didn't exist.

If you're sick of wasting your time in a dead-end job, tired of tearing things down instead of building something up, or just ready to get your hands dirty with clean, honest work, write and tell us why you'd make a worthy wife for a man who has spent the last decade in uniform.

There wasn't much to laugh at in this paragraph. Regan read it again, then got up and wandered to the kitchen to top up her glass. She'd never seen a singles ad like this one. She could see why it was going viral. If it was real, these men were something special. Who wanted to do clean, honest work these days? What kind of man was selfless enough to serve in the military instead of sponging off their girlfriends? If she'd known there were guys like this in the world, she might not have been so quick to schedule the artificial insemination appointment.

She wouldn't cancel it, though, because these guys couldn't be for real, and she wasn't waiting another minute to start her family. She had dreamed of having children ever since she was a child herself and organized pretend schools in her backyard for the neighborhood little ones. Babies loved her. Toddlers thought she was the next best thing to teddy bears. Her co-workers at the bank had never appreciated her as much as the average five-year-old did.

Further down the page there were photographs of the ranch the brothers meant to bring back to life. The land was beautiful, if overgrown, but its toppled fences and sagging buildings were a testament to its neglect. The photograph of the main house caught her eye and kept her riveted, though. A large gothic structure, it could be beautiful with the proper care. She could see why these men would dedicate themselves to returning it to its former glory. She tried to imagine what it would be like to live on the ranch with one of them, and immediately her body craved an open sunny sky—the kind you were hard pressed to see in the city. She sunk into the daydream, picturing herself sitting on a back porch sipping lemonade while her cowboy worked and the baby napped. Her husband would have his shirt off while he chopped wood, or mended a fence or whatever it was ranchers did. At the end of the day they'd fall into bed and make love until morning.

Regan sighed. It was a wonderful daydream, but it had no bearing on her life. Disgruntled, she switched over to Netflix and set up a foreign film. She fetched the bottle of wine back to bed with her and leaned against her many pillows. She'd managed to hang her small flatscreen on the opposite wall. In an apartment this tiny, every piece of furniture needed to serve double-duty.

As the movie started, Regan found herself composing messages to the military men in the Wife Wanted ad, in which she described herself as trim and petite, or lithe and strong, or horny and good-enough-looking to do the trick.

An hour later, when the film failed to hold her attention, she grabbed her laptop again. She pulled up the Wife Wanted page and reread it, keeping an eye on the foreign couple on the television screen who alternately argued and kissed.

Crazy what some people did. What was wrong with these men that they needed to advertise for wives instead of going out and meeting them like normal people?

She thought of the online dating sites she'd tried in the past. She'd had some awkward experiences, some horrible first dates, and finally one relationship that lasted for a couple of months before the man was transferred to Tucson and it fizzled out. It hadn't worked for her, but she supposed lots of people found love online these days. They might not advertise directly for spouses, but that was their ultimate intention, right? So maybe this ad wasn't all that unusual.

Most men who posted singles ads weren't as hot as these men were, though. Definitely not the ones she'd met. She poured herself another glass. A small twinge of her conscience told her she'd already had far too much wine for a single night.

To hell with that, Regan thought. As soon as she got pregnant she'd have to stay sober and sane for the next eighteen years. She wouldn't have a husband to trade off with—she'd always be the designated driver, the adult in charge, the sober, wise mother who made sure nothing bad ever happened to her child. Just this one last time she was allowed to blow off steam.

But even as she thought it, a twinge of fear wormed through her belly.

What if she wasn't good enough?

She stood up, strode the two steps to the kitchenette and made herself a bowl of popcorn. She drowned it in butter and salt, returned to the bed in time for the ending credits of the movie, and lined up *Pride and Prejudice* with Colin Firth. Time for comfort food and a comfort movie. *Pride and Prejudice* always did the trick when she felt blue. She checked the Wife Wanted page again on her laptop. If she was going to pick one of the men—which she wasn't— who would she choose?

Mason, the oldest, due to leave the Navy in a matter of weeks, drew her eye first. With his dark crew cut, hard jaw and uncompromising blue eyes he looked like the epitome of a military man. He stated his interests as ranching—of course—history, natural sciences and tactical operations, whatever the hell that was. That left her little more in-formed than before she'd read it, and she wondered what the man was really like. Did he read the newspaper in bed on Sunday mornings? Did he prefer lasagna or spaghetti? Would he listen to country music in his truck or talk radio? She stared at his photo, willing him to answer.

The next two brothers, Austin and Zane, were less fierce, but looked no less intelligent and determined. Still, they didn't draw her eye the way the way Mason did. Colt, the youngest, was blond with a grin she bet drew women like flies. That one was trouble, and she didn't need trouble.

She read Mason's description again and decided he was the leader of this endeavor. If she was going to pick one, it would be him.

But she wasn't going to pick one. She had given up all that. She'd made a promise to her imaginary child that she would not allow any chaos into its life. No dating until her baby wore a graduation gown, at the very least. She felt another twinge. Was she ready to give up men for nearly two decades? That was a long time.

It's worth it, she told herself. She had no doubt about her desire to be a mother. She had no doubt she'd be a great mom. She was smart, capable and had a good head on her shoulders. She was funny, silly and patient, too. She loved children.

She was just lousy with men.

But that didn't matter anymore. She pushed the laptop aside and returned her attention to *Pride and Prejudice*, quickly falling into an old drinking game she and Laurel had devised one night that required taking a swig of wine each time one of the actresses lifted her eyebrows in polite surprise. When she finished the bottle, she headed to the tiny kitchenette to track down another one, trilling, "Jane! Elizabeth!" at the top of her voice along with Mrs. Bennett in the film. There was no more wine, so she switched to tequila.

By the time Elizabeth Bennett discovered the miracle of Mr. Darcy's palace-sized mansion, and decided she'd been too hasty in turning down his offer of marriage, Regan had decided she too needed to cast off her prejudices and find herself a man. A hot hunk of a military man. She grabbed the laptop, fumbled with the link that would let her leave Mason Hall a message and drafted a brilliant missive worthy of Jane Austen herself.

Dear Lt. Cmdr. Hall,

In her mind she pronounced lieutenant with an "f" like the Brits in the movie onscreen.

It is a truth universally acknowledged, that a single man in possession of a good ranch, must be in want of a wife. Furthermore, it must be self-evident that the wife in question should possess certain qualities numbering amongst them riding, roping, construction, roofing, farming, market gardening, cooking, cleaning, metalworking, animal care, and—most importantly, by Heaven—small motor repair.

Seeing as I am in possession of all these qualities, not to mention many others you can only have left out through unavoidable oversight or sheer obtuseness—such as glassblowing, cheesemaking, towel origami, heraldry, hovercraft piloting, and an uncanny sense of what cats are thinking—I feel almost forced to catapult myself into your purview.

You will see from my photograph that I am most eminently and majestically suitable for your wife.

She inserted a digital photo of her foot.

In fact, one might wonder why such a paragon of virtue such as I should deign to answer such a peculiar advertisement. The truth is, sir, that I long for adventure. To get my hands dirty with clean, hard work. To build something up instead of tearing it down.

In short, you are really hot. I'd like to lick you.

Yours,
Regan Anderson

On screen, Elizabeth Bennett lifted an eyebrow. Regan knocked back another shot of Jose Cuervo and passed out.

End of Excerpt

The Cowboys of Chance Creek Series:

The Cowboy Inherits a Bride (Volume 0)
The Cowboy's E-Mail Order Bride (Volume 1)
The Cowboy Wins a Bride (Volume 2)
The Cowboy Imports a Bride (Volume 3)
The Cowgirl Ropes a Billionaire (Volume 4)
The Sheriff Catches a Bride (Volume 5)
The Cowboy Lassos a Bride (Volume 6)
The Cowboy Rescues a Bride (Volume 7)
The Cowboy Earns a Bride (Volume 8)
The Cowboy's Christmas Bride (Volume 9)

The Heroes of Chance Creek Series:

The Navy SEAL's E-Mail Order Bride (Volume 1)
The Soldier's E-Mail Order Bride (Volume 2)
The Marine's E-Mail Order Bride (Volume 3)
The Navy SEAL's Christmas Bride (Volume 4)
The Airman's E-Mail Order Bride (Volume 5)

The SEALs of Chance Creek Series:

A SEAL's Oath
A SEAL's Vow
A SEAL's Pledge
A SEAL's Consent
A SEAL's Purpose
A SEAL's Resolve
A SEAL's Devotion
A SEAL's Desire
A SEAL's Struggle
A SEAL's Triumph

The Brides of Chance Creek Series:

Issued to the Bride One Navy SEAL
Issued to the Bride One Airman
Issued to the Bride One Sniper
Issued to the Bride One Marine
Issued to the Bride One Soldier

The Turners v. Coopers Series:

The Cowboy's Secret Bride (Volume 1)
The Cowboy's Outlaw Bride (Volume 2)
The Cowboy's Hidden Bride (Volume 3)
The Cowboy's Stolen Bride (Volume 4)
The Cowboy's Forbidden Bride (Volume 5)

About the Author

With over one million books sold, NYT and USA Today bestselling author Cora Seton has created a world readers love in Chance Creek, Montana. She has twenty-eight novels and novellas currently set in her fictional town, with many more in the works. Like her characters, Cora loves cowboys, military heroes, country life, gardening, bike-riding, binge-watching Jane Austen movies, keeping up with the latest technology and indulging in old-fashioned pursuits. Visit **www.coraseton.com** to read about new releases, contests and other cool events!

Blog:

www.coraseton.com

Facebook:

www.facebook.com/coraseton

Twitter:

www.twitter.com/coraseton

Newsletter:

www.coraseton.com/sign-up-for-my-newsletter